The Essential list

✓ GPS unit
✓ Radio
✓ Waterproof matches
✓ Compass
✓ Pocketknife
✓ Rifle
✓ Bullets
✓ Cord

✓ Padlock
✓ Torch
✓ Batteries
✓ Warm waterproof jacket
✓ Gloves
✓ Beanie

violet claar

King Cobra's
Curse

Sean Willmore & Alison Reynolds

The Five Mile Press

*For Jill Veitch wildlife traveller extraordinaire
and Noel Shillong who brought India to life for me.*
AR

*Dedicated to both my father, Harry Willmore – a great storyteller,
entertainer and compassionate being who taught me creativity
through adversity, and the rangers around the world who put their
lives on the line for wildlife and this planet. Both are my heroes.*
SW

The Five Mile Press Pty Ltd
1 Centre Road, Scoresby
Victoria 3179 Australia
www.fivemile.com.au

First published 2010
Reprinted 2010

Cover design by Brad Maxwell
Cover and internal illustrations by Andrew Hopgood
Page design by TypeSkill

National Library of Australia Cataloguing-in-Publication entry:

Willmore, Sean.
King cobra's curse : decide your destiny / Sean Willmore, Alison Reynolds.
978 1 74211 793 5 (pbk.)
Willmore, Sean. Ranger in danger.
For primary school age.
Reynolds, Alison.
A823.4

This book is printed and bound in Australia at McPherson's Printing Group.
The paper is manufactured from 100% recycled material.

The journey is long.
We rangers are crusaders fighting a battle all alone in
different parts of the world.
Many of our colleagues breathe their last,
fighting this battle like unsung heroes.
I will call them Earth heroes who give their today for the
tomorrow of others.
If there is a second birth,
I will ask God to make me a ranger again and again,
so I can work for the protection of the natural heritage,
which helps humankind survive.

Paresh Porob – Ranger
Bondla Wildlife Sanctuary, Goa, India

India

TAJIKISTAN

AFGHANISTAN

disputed territory

Jammu and Kashmir

disputed territory

PAKISTAN

CHINA

Himachal Pradesh

Uttarakhand

Haryana

Punjab

Delhi

H i m a l a y a s

Arunachal Pradesh

Sikkim

NEPAL

BHUTAN

Rajasthan

Uttar Pradesh

Bihar

Assam

Meghalaya

BANGLADESH

Jharkhand

Nagaland

Madhya Pradesh

West Bengal

Manipur

Gujarat

Tripura

MYANMAR

Dadra and Nagar Haveli

Maharashtra

(Odisha) Orissa

Mizoram

Goa

Andhra Pradesh

Bay of Bengal

Chhattisgarh

Karnataka

Andaman and Nicobar Islands (India)

Arabian Sea

Tamil Nadu

Kerala

SRI LANKA

Indian Ocean

To: Ranger
From: Paresh Porob
Subject: Help!

Several Indian rangers have disappeared in the line of duty. The last one, Deepak, never returned from a regular patrol of our national park.

I fear we have a master criminal at work. One of my fellow countrymen seems prepared to do anything to make money. We need your help to stop him.

I won't lie. Your life will be in danger. I will, of course, understand if you decide not to come.

Paresh Porob

You stare at the screen, thinking. Will you put your life in danger? You've been lucky to survive your previous adventures.

If you decide you've used up your luck and you'll stay home, turn to page 2

If you decide to put your life in danger yet again, turn to page 3

You've been lucky to survive up to this point. One day your luck might run out.

You write a polite email to Paresh Porob and explain you're sorry you can't come now, but maybe you will later. You settle into your usual ranger duties. You undertake controlled burn-offs and teach park visitors about the native wildlife. Soon you forget all about India because you're achieving so much in your own national park.

Then one day you read the news headlines. Twenty-six rangers in India have disappeared, and it is rumoured that Paresh Porob is among those missing.

You feel dreadful. Next time if someone asks you for help you'll go, no matter what the danger.

2

THE END

Of course you'll put your life in danger. You're not the 'ranger in danger' for nothing.

Three days later you're gazing out through the window of an empty train compartment at the dark Indian countryside. You stretch out on what the conductor called your private sleeping berth, but what you call a long padded bench. Time to go to sleep; then in the morning your adventures will start when you meet Paresh Porob. You can't wait.

You snuggle down and drift off. Someone enters the carriage and sits on your feet so you pull them up towards you a bit. During the night the door opens again and again, but you're too tired to open your eyes.

You wake in agony; you're a human pretzel with your knees practically resting beside your ears. Six men sit where your legs should be. It's as if the one billion people who live in India are trying to cram into your train compartment.

Something splats on your head.

Turn to page 4

You look up. A hen roosts on the luggage rack next to your ranger hat. Welcome to India.

'I'm sorry,' murmurs a woman draped in an aqua sari. She's squeezed in next to seven other people on the opposite bench. 'I'm taking the bird for my brother's wedding.' She reaches across three men asleep on the floor and hands you a tissue.

'It is good luck for a bird to do its business on you,' says a small man in a dark suit with a red tie. He smiles.

You bet he wouldn't be smiling if he were the bird's target practice. You wipe your hair and look out the window at a group of elephants carrying large logs with their trunks. The mahout, or elephant handler, rides the leading elephant and jabs a long stick called an ankus into its leg.

You flinch. The ankus often has a sharp spike on the end that can puncture the elephant's skin and cause injury, tetanus and even death.

'It's all right,' murmurs the small man in the suit. 'This mahout uses an ankus without spikes. Watch how he steers the elephant with his feet, behind its ears.'

You relax. Elephants can be trained to respond to slight pressure on the back of their ears instead of being jabbed with sharp spikes and hooks.

One of the guys asleep on the floor stirs and rolls over onto his back. He's about twenty, slim with long black hair and a wispy beard.

Turn to page 6

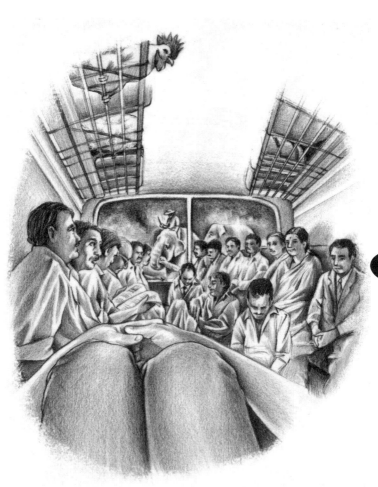

The small man starts and sweat glistens on his forehead, despite the train's efficient airconditioning.

His dark eyes watch you intently, then he nods and slips a business card out of his shirt pocket. He pulls out a pen and squiggles something on the card. His jacket sleeve slides up to reveal a piece of thin green string with three knots fastened to his wrist. It looks weird with his formal suit.

'I'm Mr Gupta. I work for the Axco Trading Company. If you need help, contact me. I foretell we'll meet again. I may have something you need.'

'Nice to meet you ...' You stop as he stands and exits the carriage.

What was that about?

'It is a wonderful thing for him to give you his card,' says the woman in the aqua sari. 'He works for one of the world's most powerful companies, based in India. It is a great stroke of luck.'

You believe people make their own luck, but who knows? You turn the card over to see what he drew. It's a king cobra in strike position, its hood flared out. Why?

Suddenly, the young guy who stirred earlier leaps up and dashes out the door.

Goosebumps creep over your body. Something's not right.

If you decide to follow the young guy, turn to page 8
If you decide not to follow him, turn to page 79

You grab your backpack, put on your ranger hat and leave the compartment.

The corridor's empty. You march along the carriage, peering inside every crowded compartment, but you spy neither Mr Gupta nor the slim young guy.

Soon you'll arrive at Fortescue Station, so you pull on your backpack. For a second, something presses against your shoulderblades.

Nobody's there.

You feel it again. Something's moving in your backpack. Carefully, you ease it off your shoulders and place it on the floor.

A door slams. You look up and see the slim young guy at the end of the corridor, outside the bathroom.

'Hey!' he yells.

You've just got enough time to see what's in the bag before he reaches you.

If you decide to open your bag, turn to page 9
If you decide to observe the bag first, turn to page 12

You unzip the flap of your backpack. Nothing, except for
your T-shirts, socks and shorts.

You slide your hand down to the bottom.

Something nips you, but it doesn't really hurt.

'Are you all right?' The young guy kneels beside you.

'What do you know about this?' you ask, staring
at him.

He looks both guilty and frightened. 'My name's Raj.
Did it bite you?'

'Did what bite me?' you ask.

He grabs your backpack and empties it. Your clothes
tumble out, along with a loosely coiled-up ball of snake.

Oh boy.

9

Turn to page 10

You recognise the steely blue hexagonal scales, and the white bands around the body of the snake. A common krait, one of the most venomous snakes in the world. Even though you feel no pain, you know that this is usual with krait bites. Soon you'll be fighting for your life.

'Why did it bite you?' asks Raj. 'They're not meant to bite during the day. They're nocturnal.'

'The dark inside the backpack would fool it.' Even though you talk calmly, terrible cramps begin to grip your stomach. 'The krait could think it was night-time. They're normally an extremely timid snake, but I probably poked it right in the head. You have to help me.'

Raj stares at you with wide, terrified eyes as you collapse on the floor. He says, 'It was just meant to be a warning for rangers to keep out of other people's business. The big boss, King Cobra, ordered me to do it.'

Was that why Mr Gupta drew the king cobra on the back of his business card? Was it a warning? You try to work it out, but pain overwhelms you and paralysis slowly creeps throughout your body. You can't move your fingers.

'Help me,' you whisper through waves of agony. It feels like a swordfish is swimming in your stomach. It hurts so much. 'Raj?'

Turn to page 11

Raj drags you along the vinyl floor towards the bathroom, but you don't feel a thing. You silently plead for someone to look out of their compartment and see you, but the little part of your brain that still works observes that the compartment doors are solid wood, except for a high window. No-one will see you unless he or she walks out into the corridor.

You try to yell, but no sound comes out. The creeping paralysis has reached your vocal cords. If you don't have treatment soon, you'll die. You need to be put on a ventilator. If left untreated, the victim of a krait bite suffocates.

The tiles of the bathroom must be cold, but your paralysed limbs feel nothing. Raj shoves you next to the hand basin, then leaves. He shuts the door.

You hear his footsteps become softer and softer as he walks away.

THE END

From page 8

You listen for sounds coming from the bag. Nothing.

You sniff. All you smell is your own sweat. You really need a shower.

You stare at the backpack. Something's definitely wriggling inside it. You listen again, more intently, and hear a faint hiss.

It's possible for a snake to bite through material, so you grab your pocketknife from your pocket and hook it into the zip fastener. The flap falls open.

The slim young guy reaches you, but leaps back as a snake glides out of your backpack. It's about a metre long with beautiful blue-grey hexagonal scales, and white bands around its body. It's a krait, one of the most venomous snakes in the world.

12

Turn to page 14

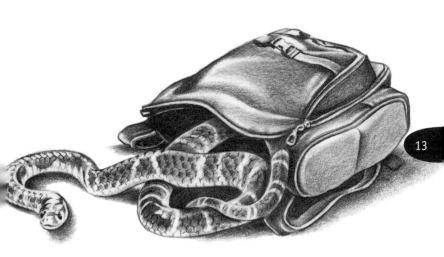

13

The krait is also one of the most timid snakes in the world.

The two of you watch it gradually coil into a loose ball, its tail flicking back and forth like the slow wag of a drowsy dog.

'They sleep during the day,' you say, conversationally.

'As if I didn't know,' sniffs the young guy. 'It was only meant as a warning; no-one wants to kill you. But I do want that business card you were given.'

He's bigger and older than you, but that doesn't mean you're not faster. You race to the end of the carriage and fling open the window. The wind slaps you in the face. You pull the card out of your pocket.

'I'll take that.' A hand squeezes your arm so tightly you expect the bones to mash. A newish-looking tattoo of a king cobra marks his forearm.

You twist away and lean out the window. The train rounds a bend and slows down; it must be approaching your station. You put your hand below the level of the window so the card won't blow back inside the train.

'Take this.' You drop the card and watch it blow against the side of the train, then fall on the tracks underneath. 'Hah!'

Something cracks your head. Pain washes over you until blackness swallows you.

Turn to page 15

From page 14

A groaning sound fills the room. Everything is white: white sheets, white walls, and a woman wearing a snowy white dress. She flicks a switch and the room explodes into light. You wince, and the groans stop. You realise that you were the one making the noise.

'You're awake at last.' She smiles as if it's the cleverest thing she's ever seen. 'You're in the hospital. That will teach you to lean out of trains and bump your head on tunnels.'

'What?'

'You don't remember?' She frowns. 'My name's Dhara.'

'I'm ...' You can't remember your name.

'Don't worry, your memory will return.' She hands you a travel folder.

You stare at it. You can't remember ever seeing it before. You open the passport and a face gazes back at you. 'Who's that?'

Silently, she hands you a mirror.

It's your face. You don't know who you are.

Turn to page 16

Three weeks later you have no headaches or pain. You also have no memory.

'The amnesia will soon pass,' Dhara says. 'Your memory will return. Maybe triggered by a sight, a smell or a noise.' She fluffs up her hair. 'I can't believe I'm meeting Paresh Porob. He's famous for all his good work. And you, you're a ranger, too. What a wonderful thing.'

You nod. You can't remember being a ranger, but your papers say you are.

'Don't worry, he'll look after you,' says Dhara.

The door swings open and a tall man strides in. He wears a ranger hat and uniform plus a face mask and gloves, so all you see is his dark eyes. 'Paresh Porob.' He taps his face mask. 'Stops the spread of animal germs.'

You stare at him. Can you spread animals' germs?

'*Agghh!*' Dhara jumps in fright as something brushes past her, before realising it's just a butterfly. 'Silly me.'

Paresh Porob whips off his hat and squashes the butterfly against the wall. He glances at his shiny gold watch, strapped on top of a surgical glove. 'Let's go.'

You observe the beautiful pale-blue spots on the butterfly's crumpled body. Why kill a common jay? Hey, you remembered the butterfly's name. 'Dhara ...'

'Cut the cackle and hurry up.' Paresh checks his watch again. 'I'll take your bag.'

Why the hurry? And how could he kill a butterfly?

If you try to stall, turn to page 17
If you leave with Paresh Porob, turn to page 62

From page 16

Paresh seems in too much of a hurry. The way he glances at his watch all the time makes you suspicious. You don't know why, but no-one can expect anybody without a memory to be able to work out anything.

'Come on,' commands Paresh. 'I'm tired of waiting for you.'

Dhara gapes at him.

'I mean, many people wait to greet you at the ranger camp – there would be so much disappointment if you were late.' His voice sounds calm, but you note how he balls his hands into fists.

'*Ouch*,' you moan. 'I don't feel too good.'

'You'll feel better back in the national park. All that nature. Marvellous for you.'

Paresh marches towards the door.

'Dhara, help me ...' You pretend to slump off the chair onto the floor.

She curls an arm around you and helps you stagger back to bed. She pulls back the sheets and you climb in.

17

Turn to page 18

'I'll feel better after a little lie down,' you murmur in a weak voice.

'Plenty of choice of beds at the ranger station. Come on.' Paresh yanks you up, forcing you to sit on the side of the bed.

'I think I'm going to be sick.' You retch loudly and lean forward. Paresh quickly withdraws his shiny new boots from the vomit zone.

Dhara picks up a pale green plastic dish and hands it to you. 'Sorry,' she says as she steps hard on Paresh's foot, but she doesn't look sorry.

Paresh's eyes flash, and you wish you could observe his face. You're positive he isn't smiling behind that mask.

Suddenly, there's a kerfuffle outside. You hear the words 'Paresh Porob'.

He freezes, then shoves Dhara aside and flings open the window, jumping out.

What the ...?

A man dressed in a ranger's uniform appears at the door. He has a huge smile on his face.

'Welcome, welcome,' he says and sweeps off his ranger's hat. 'I'm so sorry this is the first opportunity to visit, but I can't wait to take you back to the ranger station. We can begin work now you're well.'

'And who might you be?' demands Dhara.

'Beg your pardon, I should have introduced myself. I am Paresh Porob.'

Turn to page 19

'Am I losing my mind?' you ask aloud.

'Well if you are, I'm right beside you,' says Dhara.

Paresh Porob Version II, or whoever he is, rubs his wavy black hair and frowns. 'Surely you knew I was coming? I don't mean to upset either of you.'

'Prove it,' demands Dhara.

'Pardon?' This second version of Paresh Porob gazes at Dhara in amazement. 'I don't understand.'

'Show us some identification,' you say.

Paresh Porob Version II pats the side pockets of his shorts. 'Must have left my wallet in the jeep.'

'Huh,' says Dhara. 'A likely tale. Paresh Porob was just here. I'm calling security.'

'I don't wish to appear vain, but haven't you seen me on television?'

'You're a little like him,' Dhara admits, 'but the real Paresh Porob looks taller and much more handsome than you.'

'Lights, even a little make-up,' says Paresh Porob Version II, modestly.

Dhara studies him and shakes her head. 'No, the television one looks much more like the Paresh Porob who just jumped out of the window.'

'What?' Paresh Porob Version II rushes over to the window. 'We must leave.'

If you decide not to trust Paresh Porob Version II,
turn to page 20
If you decide to trust Paresh Porob Version II, turn to page 21

From page 19

Are you crazy, as well as having no memory? Of course this Paresh Porob is the real Paresh Porob.

Your basic ranger training should tell you that a real ranger would never choose to deliberately kill a butterfly like the first Paresh Porob.

You don't deserve to be a ranger in danger. It is time for you to return to your country.

THE END

Paresh scans the countryside, empty except for a few elephants in the distance. 'No sign of him. Will we leave?'

You leap up and grab your backpack.

'Are you crazy?' demands Dhara. 'You can't go with this impostor.'

'I believe him. The first Paresh Porob was no ranger. I don't remember much, but I do know that no true ranger would deliberately kill a butterfly. Rangers protect animals, they don't destroy them.'

'Well said,' says Paresh Porob Version II. 'We must try and find the impostor.'

'But the other Paresh looked much more like the one on the television.'

'Dhara, we couldn't even see his face under the mask. His new boots should have made me suspicious. No ranger ever has boots that new and shiny.' You wonder how you know that. It's as if your memory swims around your head like a fish. You keep nearly catching the fish, but it slips away too fast.

'Nice to meet you, Paresh Porob.' You shake his hand.

'You too. Want to leave now?' Paresh picks up your backpack.

'Thanks for everything, Dhara.'

She pats your back. 'Good luck. If you need help, contact me.'

Something wriggles in your brain.

Turn to page 22

21

Someone else said that to you. A picture of a white card swims into your mind. And a man. He disappears. You screw up your eyes to try to remember. No, it's gone.

'Are you okay? Should you stay in hospital a few more days?' Paresh studies you.

'No, I want to leave now,' you say. 'Bye, Dhara. I really am fine.'

It's fantastic to be outside. The morning sun sparkles on the dew as the jeep travels through open grassland. Huge, jagged, snow-peaked mountains cut into the deep blue sky.

'Grab my wallet and check my ID,' says Paresh. 'It's near your feet.'

'No need for that,' you say.

'I don't want any doubts if we're to work together.'

You lean down and pick up the blue wallet. A photo ID of Paresh Porob grins at you. 'You're definitely the real Paresh Porob.'

'That's a relief – to know I am who I think I am.'

You grin, but you're jealous. You know your name but you don't know who the real you is. You blink and wipe your eyes with the back of your hand.

Paresh glances at you. 'You'll remember soon,' he says, soothingly.

You clear your throat. 'I know. Anyway, who was the fake you?'

Turn to page 24

A pained look crosses Paresh's face as he watches the road. 'I suspect a certain master criminal, but I can't understand why you're involved and why he visited you in hospital. It makes no sense.'

'Paresh,' you say hesitantly, 'I think this all started when I was on the train.'

'You remember something that happened there?' asks Paresh, hopefully.

You shake your head. 'No, but even though I can't remember, I don't think I was a stupid person before the amnesia. I can't be too silly if I'm a ranger.'

Paresh nods his head. 'I can tell you are a good, intelligent person.'

You continue, 'I believe I would only lean out of a railway carriage if I had an excellent reason. I wouldn't risk doing something that dangerous and stupid unless I had no other choice. Also, one of my arms was very bruised but no-one knows why.'

Turn to page 25

The jeep slows as a reddish-brown cow wanders across the road. Paresh brakes as another cow, then another cow, saunters in front of the car. Soon a whole herd gathers. They moo and bellow so loudly you want to cover your ears with your hands.

'Paresh!' you shout. It's so noisy your head hurts.

'What?' he screams back.

'Someone wants me dead.'

Paresh shakes his head and shrugs.

This is hopeless. You need to tell Paresh that you fear for your life.

If you jump out of the jeep and try to push the cows off the road, turn to page 26

If you sit quietly beside Paresh and wait for the cows to move on, turn to page 31

You fling the door open and jump out. About twenty cows clog up the road.

'Move!' you yell. *'Go-ooorrrrn.'*

The cows stand still and moo even louder, if that's possible.

'Giddy-up. Giddy-up.'

Obviously these cows don't understand English. A huge one with reddish eyes trots towards you and snorts. Long strands of mucus decorate your ranger shirt. The cow doesn't seem to like you much.

A few large sticks lie scattered by the roadside. You pick one up and wave it in the air. 'I'm not crazy about you either!' you scream.

The cow swings around and evacuates its bowels right near your boots.

'Get moving ...' You stop and listen. There's a different noise above the racket of the cows. It's a siren.

Turn to page 28

A police motorbike with a sidecar zooms down the road. It screams to a stop about thirty metres away and a policeman dismounts. He beckons to you and takes out a large yellow notebook.

You jog up to him. 'I'm trying to move the cows for you, sir.' It's quieter here, away from the cows.

'Please climb into the sidecar,' he answers.

You peer through the dark shade on his helmet to see if he's smiling. Why would you want to climb into his sidecar? He must be joking. You smile nervously.

Paresh gallops up. 'What's this about?'

'Step aside, ranger. My superiors have instructed me to conduct surveillance on all cars leaving the hospital. I'm only interested in this young person here.' He gestures at you and flips open the notebook. 'You are charged with attacking cows. In this part of India, cow attacking is an offence. An offence punishable by a jail sentence.'

Turn to page 29

'The cow attacked *me*. Look at the state of my shirt.'

'This ranger committed no such attack. Rangers protect animals. They would never be cruel to any creature,' Paresh says to the policeman.

The flash of a camera blinds you. 'Now I have photographic evidence. The offender was seen brandishing a weapon and attacking cows mercilessly.'

You drop the stick. 'I didn't touch them. I just waved it about a bit, and it didn't work. Look at all of them.'

You swing around. The road's empty. Those rotten cows have slunk away.

The policeman grips his pen tightly and tries to write. He clicks his tongue and removes his right motorcycle glove. You stare at the black tattoo on the back of his hand.

'But no cow was harmed, I promise,' says Paresh. 'We'll be on our way ...'

You hear Paresh arguing, but allow yourself to be led to the sidecar. Pain fills your skull. That tattoo on the policeman's hand. It's a king cobra. Your head swirls as memories crowd in. Jumbled images flash through your mind. The slim young guy with the wispy beard.

The motorbike throbs into life.

'This is a mistake!' yells Paresh. 'Wait!'

'Ring Mr Gupta!' you scream to Paresh. 'He works for the Axco Trading Company. He offered to help me.'

Turn to page 30

From page 29

The motorbike stops at a police station. You're fingerprinted, photographed and three hours later a guard shows Paresh inside. His mouth is a narrow line and he looks so furious you expect to see steam blow out of his ears. 'They're determined to charge you unless you depart the country immediately.'

The guard marches out and locks the door. Paresh grins. 'It's a miracle. Mr Gupta has agreed to help us. He works for the most powerful and dubious company in all of India, the Axco Trading Company. He suspects that King Cobra, the master criminal, is the boss of Axco. Mr Gupta also secretly arranged your release.'

You smile. 'My memory returned when I saw the policeman's tattoo.'

Paresh grasps your hand. 'Your memory is back!'

You shush him. 'We don't know how much time we have. I'll tell you everything that happened on the train.'

One question strikes you. 'Paresh, I thought it was weird that Mr Gupta, in his smart suit, wore a cheap piece of green string with three knots around his wrist.'

The guard bangs on the door. Paresh pulls out a piece of thin green string. 'It's a sign of those who support us rangers in our quest to protect the natural world. Tie three knots, and with each knot make a wish. When the string falls off, your wishes will come true.'

You think for ages before you tie the three knots. Even after you return home, you're determined to continue the fight for rangers and their families.

THE END

From page 25

You'll have to wait it out; then you can talk to Paresh. You watch as one cow casts a scornful glance at the jeep and plops down on the road.

Someone, or a dog, at least, should be here to round up the cows. A scrap of memory clicks in your brain. In India the cow is respected as a sacred beast and allowed to roam freely. Cow facts swirl around in your head. These cows all have the tall, skinny haunches of the dairy cow because they provide milk rather than meat. 'Is it true that you can be jailed for killing a cow?' you ask.

'Yes. In Delhi, cows are one of the greatest traffic hazards. People known as cowboys are hired to catch them gently and load them into trucks that transport them to cow reserves. Unfortunately, the cows, which often have rather sharp horns, seem to know the sound of the transport trucks and perform a type of cow ballet to keep the cowboys at bay.' Paresh chuckles. 'I've seen many a grown man pirouetted into the gutter.'

The cow struggles up from the ground and wanders into the tall grass at the side of the road. It has white splotches above its hooves. You smile; they look like surgical gloves or booties. Then it strikes you. Why did the impostor at the hospital need to wear gloves as well as a face mask?

'Paresh, the impostor wanted to hide his hands.'

'I fear I know who it is, but I don't understand how he knows of you.'

Turn to page 32

Your heart pounds. You shiver despite the blazing sun.

Paresh turns on the ignition and the jeep creeps past the last cow. He sighs. 'He's known as King Cobra. No-one knows his real name. He trades everything, he doesn't care what: endangered animals, plastic buckets. He just wants to make money. I suspect he runs a company, but I haven't been able to name it.'

'Why the name King Cobra?' you ask.

'People believe he exerts a strange power over cobras. I suspect he rips out their fangs so they can't bite him, thus shortening their lives because eventually they starve to death. Cobras need the venom to help break down meat so they can digest it.' Paresh brushes his finger across the back of his hand. You see a piece of green knotted string on his wrist. 'He has a tattoo of a king cobra here.'

Images flash through your mind. Green string and the picture of a king cobra jumble together. You stutter, 'I ... I ... I've seen it before.'

'The tattoo?'

'Both. But I can't remember where. I think they were on two different people.'

'Let us hope you're correct. We've had reports that those who work for King Cobra sport such a tattoo. The green string is worn to show support for rangers.'

Suddenly, a man appears by the roadside. He flags you down, looking desperate.

Turn to page 33

The man runs to the jeep. 'You must help. A leopard fell down the well. A poacher shot it. The other villagers want to kill it and sell it to the poacher. Please.'

You and Paresh grab your backpacks and leap out of the jeep.

The nearby village consists of a few houses built of mud bricks. Each house is painted a different colour: pink, blue and yellow. Mud houses are the most common form of house in India. You shake your head. How did you know that?

'Hurry!' shouts Paresh over his shoulder.

A crowd gathers around a circle of stones: the village well.

You dash to the well, promptly slip in a wet puddle, and bang your head on an upturned bucket.

Everyone laughs and you jump up, pretending to laugh too, but inside you cringe. So much for looking like a capable ranger. And your head hurts, but not as badly as it did when your head struck the tunnel. The tunnel!

Everything clicks back in your mind. You remember the train, the young guy with the wispy beard, Mr Gupta. Your memory has returned with the bang on your head.

'Paresh,' you say urgently. 'I remember everything. My memory's back.'

He smiles, but points down the well. 'I'm glad, but I don't know what to do here.'

Turn to page 34

You shine your torch down the well and see the broad head of a leopard. Its tawny wet coat, with irregular dark rosettes, gleams in the light as it thrashes around in the water. Luckily, leopards not only swim, but they also like water.

How do you remove a panicking, possibly injured leopard from a well? Leopards are well-known jumpers, but the water level is seven metres down, and the leopard isn't on solid ground. What else do you know about leopards that could help you?

They're incredibly strong and can drag prey up to three times their body weight. Leopards usually attack and kill by a bite to the back of the neck. You pull your jacket collar up and aim your torch on the leopard. Red blood discolours the well water. That isn't good for either the leopard or you. Leopards are extremely dangerous when injured.

34

Turn to page 35

You gaze down at the injured animal. Who would do that to an animal? 'What about the poacher?'

'We'll work on that later.' Paresh's voice sounds grim. 'Now we concentrate on the leopard. We'll make a sort of rope harness and haul it up.'

He opens his backpack and pulls out some cord.

'No way will this leopard hold still and keep its claws retracted for us,' you say. 'How can we get close without injury?'

'I guess it's a he by the size. The male is a third larger than the female, and this is a big boy. We need this.' Paresh holds up a tranquilliser gun and hands you some darts. 'Take the spare darts.'

You tuck the darts into your pocket and help Paresh tie ropes to a tree with heart-shaped leaves. It's a peepul tree, which some people claim is the longest-living tree in the world. A tree planted in 288 BCE still grows today. You hope the leopard has a long life too.

Paresh abseils down the well. Quickly you follow him.

35

Turn to page 36

From page 35

'Better keep out of the scratch zone,' you say, although the poor leopard doesn't look as if it will be doing any amazing three-metre vertical jumps today. You brace your feet against the rocky sides of the well.

You shine your torch down and the leopard gazes up at you. The pupils of its amber eyes shrink to pinpricks in the light. You remember hearing claims that a leopard named the 'Man-eater of Panar' was responsible for 400 deaths in the 1930s and 1940s. It was injured, so unable to catch wild prey. Then there was the 'Leopard of Rudraprayag', which killed 125 people between 1918 and 1926. It was a sick, very old leopard, so the soft flesh of unguarded humans was easier for it to catch and eat. You almost wish your memory hadn't returned. There's a definite pattern of injured leopards killing humans.

You remind yourself that it's extremely rare for leopards to attack humans, but suddenly you're shaky and need to wipe your sweaty hands on your shorts. The walls of the well seem to press in on you, and you want to throw up. It wasn't that long ago you were seriously ill in hospital. Maybe it would be better if you climbed out of the well.

If you decide to climb out of the well, turn to page 38
If you decide to stay down in the well, turn to page 44

Your head spins. This isn't good. 'I'm sorry, Paresh, but I need to breathe. I feel as if I'll suffocate in this well.'

'Take slow, deep breaths,' orders Paresh. 'You'll be fine.'

The leopard hisses and the sound whirls around and around. You lift your hands to cover your ears and nearly fall off your rope. Your heart jumps as you realise how stupid that was. You could have died.

'I'm no good to you in this state.' You brace yourself against the stone wall and slowly climb up it.

'Wait,' says Paresh.

You heave yourself up over the lip of the well and look back down. 'I'll be back in a minute, once I'm rested and not giddy.'

38

The crowd of people draws away, and you're not sure but someone may have whispered the word 'coward'. You walk across the clearing around the village to the edge of the forest and lie on the grass. Your heartbeat returns to normal as you stare at the leaves of the overhead tree. A branch bends down slightly.

Turn to page 39

You peer up into the tree. Among the tightly bunched leaves, something moves, but you can't distinguish a shape. You hear a cough.

You know you didn't cough. You also know, thanks to your returned memory, that a cough is often the sound a leopard makes before it attacks. Leopards are meant to be solitary animals unless they're part of a breeding pair, when the male and female leopard travel together for a time. You also know that a leopard spends much of its time resting and sleeping up in the branches of trees.

All right. You can get out of this. Just because there could be a female leopard above your head is no reason to panic.

You freeze so the leopard won't see you as a threat. Leopards normally prefer smaller prey than a human, so hopefully it isn't hungry and looking for dinner in a hurry.

The villagers gather around the well again, but if you yell out you might upset the leopard. You stare at the branches overhead. You spot something black. The barrel of a rifle pokes out through the leaves, aimed directly at your head.

Turn to page 40

From page 39

Suddenly, a tall man springs down from the tree.

'We meet again,' he says, as he throws a lit cigarette on the grass.

Without thinking you jump up and stamp it out. He grabs you from behind and pulls an arm tightly around your neck. You struggle and he squeezes his arm tighter around your neck, until black spots float in front of your eyes. You stop fighting; you're trapped.

'Help!' you scream.

A few of the villagers run towards you, then stop.

'If anyone tries to interfere, my cobras will hunt you down,' shouts your attacker.

You know who he is, even without a face mask and gloves. You recognise his voice. 'The fake Paresh Porob,' you say.

'I prefer King Cobra,' he replies.

'Paresh!' you yell.

His head appears above the rim of the well. 'Let him go!' he yells.

In answer, King Cobra points the rifle at him. 'Either of you move and this baby goes off.'

The man who flagged you down on the road runs towards you.

'Stop!' you shout. 'He means it.'

Turn to page 42

'You're smarter than you look,' remarks King Cobra. 'Now what will we do with you two rangers? Should I wait until you pull the leopard out of the well so I can sell it, then push you down the well, or should I make you jump into the well straightaway?'

Seconds tick past. Somehow you must escape and catch King Cobra. It would be easy, except he's the one with the large rifle and he has his arm clamped tightly around your throat. You don't have a gun, or a knife or even a tranquilliser gun. Hold on: you mightn't have the gun, but you do have some darts. You need a distraction.

You lift your hand slightly and beckon to Paresh. He climbs out of the well and takes a few steps forwards.

'Stop!' shouts King Cobra.

One of the villagers, then another, creeps forward.

King Cobra swings his rifle from one to the next. 'Stop or else,' he orders.

You slip your hand into your pocket and grab a tranquilliser dart.

'Why are you wriggling?' he demands.

You reach behind him and jab his bottom as hard as you can.

Turn to page 43

From page 42

'*Aaaggghhh!*' King Cobra slumps to the ground.

You snatch his rifle as Paresh and the crowd race over.

A small cobra crawls out of King Cobra's shirt. The crowd gasps and steps back. Paresh grabs a stick and pokes the snake gently. You can tell by his skill that he's done a snake-handling course.

The cobra opens its mouth. 'As I suspected, this beast removed the cobra's fangs. He has no power over cobras. He mutilates them.' Paresh removes a cotton bag from the jeep and pops the cobra into it. 'We'll take it to a cobra rehabilitation unit, where it will be force-fed so it doesn't starve, and if it's lucky, its fangs will grow back so it can be released into the wild again.'

The villagers tie up King Cobra while you radio for help.

'We've still got something to do,' says Paresh, pointing to the well. 'Only if you feel up to it. I won't judge. You've proved yourself to be a very brave ranger.'

Suddenly, you know this time you won't feel weird down the well. Everything should go according to plan. And that's exactly what happens. You and Paresh pull the tranquillised leopard out of the well and deliver it to a nature reserve for treatment. The cobra and leopard both recover. King Cobra doesn't fare so well: he'll be in jail until he's a very old man. Everyone in jail calls him by his real name, Apu Bahm – get it?

THE END

'You look as if you need this more than the leopard.'
Paresh hands you the tranquilliser gun. You grin, but
your insides churn with fear. 'Be careful. There's only
one tranquilliser dart in the gun, and a couple in your
pocket. I'll make a rope harness for the leopard before
we descend further.'

You nod and aim the gun at the leopard.

You jump when the leopard coughs. The walls of
the well magnify the sound. You wish you didn't know
that leopards have an extremely acute sense of hearing,
and use coughing as a form of communication with
each other.

You shine your torch up to the well entrance,
expecting to see another leopard peering down at you.

Nothing, except the worried face of the man who
flagged down the jeep.

Turn to page 45

You grip the tranquilliser gun. The gun works by compressed gas; the gas in the gun propels a dart that injects anaesthetic into the animal, causing it to relax and go to sleep almost immediately. It's silent, to reduce animal stress. The leopard's already stressed enough by the well and its wound.

It hardly stirs. It may be tired, or it may be suffering life-threatening blood loss from a gunshot wound. It doesn't resemble a man-eater. It doesn't look capable of swatting a fly. This leopard needs to be rescued fast.

Blood dribbles from its mouth. It could be due to internal injuries from the poacher's gun. You lean forward and aim the torch directly at its head.

45

The leopard tucks its head down, so you can't see its mouth.

If you decide to take a slightly closer look, turn to page 46
If you decide to stay where you are, turn to page 49

You lower yourself another half a metre down the well. The leopard stays still, as if it's unaware of your presence. It must feel horrible. If you could assess where the wound site is, that could save time later when you apply first aid.

Centimetre by centimetre you lower yourself. It lifts its head again and you can see that no more blood dribbles from its mouth, so hopefully there are no internal injuries. You observe how blood oozes from a site near the leopard's tail. It could be a superficial wound from a gunshot.

'Hey,' whispers Paresh. 'What are you thinking? Get back up here.'

'On my way ...'

A wet, furry paw and lethal-looking claws flash near you. Needle-sharp pains pierce your leg.

'Use the tranquilliser gun!' screams Paresh.

Excruciating pain radiates out from your left leg. The pain is so bad you let the abseil rope slacken in your hands and you glide into the water.

Turn to page 47

Paresh looks very far away. It enters your mind that leopards sometimes pretend to climb a tree, so that the monkey in the tree will jump onto the ground to flee. Then the scared monkey turns into lunch. Leopards are extremely cunning.

You're proof of that. You could have sworn the leopard was defenceless from blood loss. Now it's you who suffers from blood loss.

Somehow you manage to tread water with one leg, and you cover the back of your neck with your hands. That's where the leopard attacks. You brace yourself.

Something drifts over your face and you can't see anymore.

'Grab hold of this,' commands a voice.

You feel as if you're flying.

Then blackness.

Turn to page 48

47

From page 47

'How are you feeling now?'

You know that voice. You open your eyes. 'Dhara?'

'Welcome back – I suppose. I warned you not to go with that Paresh Porob. Here you are again, with a mauled leg.'

'Paresh saved my life.'

'After risking it in the first place. Not that he isn't an extremely admirable man.' She fusses around you, tucking in your sheet, smoothing your pillow.

There is a knock at the door. Dhara opens it and you hear muffled voices. 'All right,' you hear her say.

Paresh sits beside you. 'Good to see you awake.'

You grip his hand. 'Thank you. Tell me, what about the leopard?'

'No good.' He looks down at his hands. 'But when we did the autopsy we discovered a bullet in the heart; it would have died regardless.'

'It was still alive when I fell in the water. Why didn't it attack me?'

'I took off my shirt and threw it over both your heads because covering the eyes often calms an animal. The leopard did quieten and I dragged you out. Tomorrow you go back to your country, but you can return to India when you recover and we'll continue our quest for King Cobra.'

'It won't be too late?' you ask.

'Alas, King Cobra shows no signs of going away.'

You shake his hand. 'That's a promise. I'll be back.'

THE END

Suddenly, the leopard lunges up. Its legs scrabble at the well's sides as it searches for a foothold. It falls back and thrashes around in the water. Lucky you waited.

The splashing stops and everything's silent except for Paresh's muttering as he knots the ropes to make a harness. The leopard's head slides under the water.

'Paresh,' you say.

The leopard's head bobs above the water again, but how much longer will it stay afloat? It needs to be rescued. If you tranquillise it now, you and Paresh could have him out of the well in about a minute.

49

Turn to page 50

'Paresh,' you say, 'he's not going to last much longer.'

'Nearly finished. Soon I'll have a safe, secure harness,' he answers.

The leopard's head starts to dip under the water again. You see a paw lying flat on the water's surface. A perfect target.

The leopard looks up at you. Should you shoot it now or wait until Paresh tells you to? Paresh hasn't observed the animal as closely as you have. This leopard's struggling and if it sinks under the water again, it might be for the last time ever.

50

If you shoot him now, turn to page 52
If you wait, turn to page 56

Time to use the tranquilliser gun. All those hours of
target practice as part of ranger training will finally
pay off.

You fire the gun.

Bullseye. The leopard slumps forward into the water.

'No!' screams Paresh.

Desperately, you swing yourself down, but there's
no sign of the leopard.

You plunge into the freezing water and dive deep.
You stretch your hands out and search for the leopard's
body. Your lungs burn as you try again and again.

A hand grabs your shoulder and heaves you to
the surface.

52

Turn to page 53

'It's gone,' says Paresh. 'It would have drowned almost immediately.'

You feel sick. It's all your fault. Leopards are a critically endangered species. As a ranger you're committed to the protection of animals. You didn't think. You were so proud of being a good shot that you went for it.

'We all make mistakes,' says Paresh. 'You'll know next time that someone needs to hold the leopard's head above the water.'

The *rat-a-tat-tat* of a machine gun rings out.

'The poacher, Paresh!' You pull yourself up the abseiling rope. 'This time we'll stop them.'

A crowd gathers as you and Paresh climb out of the well. 'The poacher,' says Paresh. 'Where is he?'

Everyone stares at the ground. 'Which direction did the gunshots come from?' you ask.

The crowd murmurs, and is then quiet.

'We must go,' says Paresh.

'But we need to find out where the poacher is,' you say.

'They won't tell us anything. Don't you understand? They fear this poacher, but they also need his money. Didn't you see the motorbikes? Someone bought them for the village.'

'Looking for me?' yells a voice.

You know that voice: the impostor Paresh Porob.

Turn to page 54

A tall man strides out of the forest. He looks like a ranger in his ranger uniform, but no ranger would drape three cobras around his neck, or point a machine gun at you. He marches towards you and Paresh. 'Chop, chop. Where's that leopard? I thought you would have rescued it by now so I could sell it. Lots of money in leopard parts. I've even got a market for the claws.' A king cobra tattoo decorates each of his hands.

'King Cobra,' hisses Paresh. 'You're like a curse that's spread through our land. You trade anything as long as you make money. You bribe people; whatever it takes.'

'Well, you're the only one complaining here,' says King Cobra. He gazes at the crowd. 'Any complaints? How are the motorbikes that I bought the village?'

No-one says a word. All you hear is a gentle hiss from one of the cobras.

'Now then, you've work to do. Haul up that leopard for me. It will weigh a tonne, all waterlogged and soggy.'

Paresh starts to shake his head, but you say, 'All right. I know when I'm beaten.'

Paresh gives you a questioning look, but joins you at the well where you pretend to pull on a rope. Minutes tick past. 'You know we radioed for reinforcements,' you say.

'I'll be gone long before then,' replies King Cobra, but he glances at his watch.

Paresh shuffles across to the tree and tightens the rope.

Turn to page 55

'Heavens!' shouts King Cobra. 'Can you be any slower, Paresh Porob? I'm always hearing reports that you're so dynamic and smart. You look much better on TV.'

Paresh ignores him and tests each of the ropes.

'Let me do it, you amateurs,' says King Cobra. He rushes to the well and peers in. 'I can't even see the leopard.'

'Come closer. Climb up onto the lip of the well and you'll see,' you say.

King Cobra leaps up onto the edge of the well, his machine gun in his hand. Quickly you push him in.

Splash! 'Let me out! It's murder, pushing me in with a leopard,' he yells.

'A dead leopard,' you murmur. Guilt sweeps over you.

Paresh grips your hand. 'By catching King Cobra, you have saved many, many leopards, and many other animals.'

'How touching,' sneers King Cobra. 'If you don't get me out, I'll catch a chill.' A huge sneeze reverberates around the well.

'Lucky the cobras have no ears or they would be deafened,' you say.

Paresh stands on the well's edge. 'King Cobra, you'll catch more than a cold. You'll catch years and years of jail.' He turns to you. 'Thank you from all my heart and the heart of my country.'

The crowd bursts into loud cheers. 'Hip hip hooray!'

THE END

The leopard's chin rests just above the surface of the water. He's about to sink.

'Paresh, hurry up,' you urge.

'Right.' Paresh holds out a knotted harness. 'We'll slip this over his head and body.'

You aim the gun.

'Wait,' says Paresh. 'One of us needs to climb down, so that when the anaesthetic works we can hold the leopard's head above the water, or else it will drown.'

You pass the gun to Paresh. 'I'll grab its head. You're more experienced.'

'Are you sure?' asks Paresh.

You nod and he hands you the rope harness. You're going down.

56

Turn to page 57

You slither down the stone wall of the well until you're just out of the leopard's strike range. You try not to remember that an injured leopard is more likely to attack a human.

You test the abseiling rope to make sure it's securely tied around your middle, then you slowly drop down and stretch out your arms. This is the most vulnerable moment of your life.

'Lucky you're not eating,' says Paresh.

'Why?' you ask.

'There's an old Tanzanian proverb, "He who dines with the leopard is liable to be eaten."'

'Thanks, Paresh,' you mutter.

57

'I'll shoot on the count of three, then five seconds later you dive down,' he says. 'Remember, grab the leopard's head.'

You nod and stare downwards. The leopard spots you and stretches its mouth wide to reveal eight razor-sharp, five-centimetre-long canines.

'One, two, three ...' counts Paresh.

Here goes.

Turn to page 58

'Now!' yells Paresh.

The leopard slumps and you dive down. You gasp when you hit the freezing water, but you still grab the head of the anaesthetised leopard.

The leopard's weight yanks down your abseiling rope, but you manage to brace yourself against the wall of the well and hold steady.

Quickly you loop the harness over the leopard.

'Well done,' Paresh shouts from the top of the well as he disconnects his rope and throws it down to you. 'Catch.'

You tie the rope to the leopard's harness, and it slowly rises out of the water. You climb out of the well, and the crowd helps you and Paresh hoist the leopard up. Leopards weigh up to seventy-six kilograms, so adding the weight of the water, this leopard feels like it weighs a tonne.

You and Paresh lie exhausted next to the sleeping leopard beside the well. Paresh injects the antivenene to counteract the effects of the tranquilliser. The leopard snores just like a pet cat; you can't believe that it's such a strong and dangerous animal.

Then it hits you. You've got a problem.

Turn to page 59

'Hey, Paresh.'

'Hmm,' he murmurs. He's half asleep.

'How many tranquilliser darts do we have?'

'The ones you've got in your pocket,' he says.

'I think the leopard's about to wake up.'

Paresh jumps up. 'We need to radio for help. I can't believe I forgot this. Perhaps if you inject the poor animal with another dart, then we'll wait a while to give it more antivenene. That way, the other rangers will have more time to arrive and pick up the leopard, before it fully wakes up.'

Suddenly, the leopard stretches out a paw. You and Paresh jump back.

'Quick, the tranquilliser dart,' he says.

You snatch it out of your pocket and take aim.

The leopard leaps up. You and Paresh watch amazed as it races back into the forest.

'The injury must not have been too bad,' says Paresh. 'I've seldom seen a leopard run so fast. It's as if it's on a mission.'

A moment later something crashes through the trees. You brace yourself. Hold on, it's a someone, not a something. It's the fake Paresh Porob, aka King Cobra.

'Help!' he screams. 'You villagers owe your lives to me.'

Everyone watches, stunned.

There's a snarling sound, and a leopard pads out of the trees.

Turn to page 60

From page 59

The fake Paresh Porob darts across to the nearest car, the ranger jeep, and slams the door. You watch him desperately push down the door locks. As if a leopard can open a doorhandle.

The leopard chases him and, from nearly six metres away, it leaps onto the roof of the jeep.

'He'll get away.' You can't believe it after all that's happened.

'Not necessarily,' says Paresh, swinging the car keys in his hand. 'Let's summon help, then we'll question him about the missing rangers. Look how he kidnapped you.'

King Cobra looks terrified as the leopard hugs the jeep.

'I should radio straightaway for backup.' Paresh pulls out the radio.

'Definitely,' you say.

'But I might just pack up our ropes and check on the tranquilliser gun first. We might need it later for the leopard. Look what happened when I didn't follow protocol, and the leopard nearly woke up.'

'Sometimes it's not good to rush,' you say, smiling, as King Cobra screams from inside the jeep. 'And King Cobra isn't going anywhere.'

THE END

It's weird to be outside after being stuck in hospital. You stop at a pond and breathe deeply. Something stirs in you; bits of your memory dance in your head. The pond flowers are called lotuses. You sniff their sweet, fresh aroma.

'I think I remember reading that lotus flowers help rid people of feelings of negativity. Do you believe it's true?' you ask.

Paresh Porob shrugs. 'Who cares? The car's over here.'

You gasp. It's a brand-new, top-of-the-range, four-wheel-drive Mercedes with gleaming hub caps.

'Get in,' instructs Paresh.

You climb in and sink back in the leather seats. 'Our ranger jeeps aren't anything like this,' you say. 'Hey, I remembered something else.'

Paresh grunts and stares straight ahead. Oh well, if he doesn't want to talk that's okay with you, but you can't help but think that he needs a good sniff of the anti-negativity-promoting lotus flowers.

Turn to page 63

You gaze out the windows at the open grasslands.
A mule-like animal gallops alongside you, keeping pace
with the seventy kilometres per hour you're travelling in
the four-wheel drive. A memory clicks in your brain: it's
called a wild ass or khur. 'Look, Paresh. A wild ass.'

He slams on the brakes, quickly picks up a
BlackBerry and taps something into it. 'If you see
anything else endangered or rare, let me know.'

'Sure. Hey, did you notice that I remembered
something? My memory is returning.' You stop as Paresh
doesn't even glance at you, but starts up the car. It's
very hard to converse with someone who ignores you
and wears a face mask.

The grasslands turn into woodland and he swings
onto a small dirt road. He slows the jeep and rips off his
face mask. 'That's better. We're nearly home.'

You watch for animals as you remember that native
animals tend to group near ranger camps, as somehow
they seem to know that they are safe there. You listen;
you can't even hear a bird. That's strange.

The four-wheel drive pulls up next to two trucks
parked by the road. 'Get out,' he orders. 'We go along
this trail and we're there.'

The trail is overgrown; it looks as if no-one ever
uses it. 'How come ...'

Crash! You collapse to the ground.

63

Turn to page 64

Your head spins and you feel a sort of click in your brain. Suddenly memories start flowing back. You remember the train. You remember struggling with the slim young guy with the wispy beard. You study Paresh.

'Whoopsie.' Paresh picks up a length of fishing line. 'I forgot to warn you. We stretch it across the path in case poachers or others who wish us harm try to sneak up on our camp. I automatically step over the traps now, without thinking.'

This sounds bizarre to you. You need time to think. 'I need to sit for a second.'

Paresh sits beside you on a large flat rock. Five crickets dance on the stones by your feet. You sense movement and spot a chameleon lizard, its natural colours blending into the colours of the rocky path. You study how the top and bottom eyelids join together, and the pupil is just visible through a tiny pinhole. It stares at the crickets near your and Paresh's legs. The chameleon turns a bright green; that means it's excited.

'You might want to move your legs,' you say, pointing to the chameleon. 'I reckon it's about to have lunch.'

'Why would I be scared of a lizard? I'm too far away from it anyway.'

You look at Paresh. As a ranger, he should know a certain fact about chameleons.

If you're suspicious of him and decide to flee, turn to page 65
If you're suspicious but think fleeing is overreacting,
turn to page 66

Something is definitely not right about Paresh Porob. All your instincts scream at you to flee. You know what the chameleon's going to do in about five seconds. This should create enough of a diversion for you to escape.

You yawn and flop your arms as though you're relaxing, while you brace your leg muscles ready to escape.

You watch the cricket jump on Paresh's bare leg.

A second later, you catch a flicker of movement.

'*Aaaaggghhh!*' yells Paresh. 'What was that? Something sticky attacked my leg!'

You leap up and run into the woodland. You see a path, but you veer off to the left, afraid to use the paths in case any more trick wires lie there. As a ranger, Paresh should definitely know that the sticky tongue of the chameleon is often longer than its body and that it shoots it out to catch its prey, in this case a cricket.

Thank you, chameleon, you think, for giving me enough time to escape.

A clump of wood flies out of a tree just to your right. A second later you hear a gunshot.

In the distance you hear an engine.

If you run deeper into the forest, turn to page 69
If you run towards the engine, turn to page 72

A cricket jumps on Paresh's leg.

'*Aaaaggghhh!*' he screams a second later. 'What was that?'

'The chameleon's sticky tongue. You know how its tongue is often as long or longer than its body,' you say.

'Quite right,' says Paresh. 'I wanted to test your skills.'

He shoves his hand in his pocket and withdraws a tiny pistol. 'And I also notice you've regained your memory. When were you going to share that?'

He sticks two gloved fingers in his mouth, then pulls them out, yanking off the surgical gloves. 'No need for them now,' he says. He sticks his fingers back into his mouth and whistles.

You gasp. A huge king cobra tattoo decorates each of his hands.

He holds one out to you. 'Now I can introduce myself properly. I'm King Cobra, aka master criminal according to you rangers. I prefer international businessman.'

Six thugs appear and cart you off to a dark pit. They toss you in.

You plummet down and land on something soft.

Turn to page 67

'*Ooof*,' says someone in a weak voice. 'You nearly flattened me.'

It's practically black, but you can distinguish the shapes of bodies.

A hand reaches out and grab yours. 'Welcome, I'm Deepak ...'

'The missing ranger?' you ask. Weak laughter surrounds you.

'We're all missing rangers: thirty-five of us,' says Deepak. 'This is the pit where that fiend King Cobra throws us. Sometimes he orders us to be fed, sometimes he does not.'

Dread creeps through you.

'Don't worry,' says Deepak. 'Paresh Porob will find us. He'll never give up.'

Turn to page 68

From page 67

Weeks pass. You help Deepak mark each passing day by scratching a groove with a stone into the rocky pit wall.

One day you hear a noise. A body is flung into the pit. It's still breathing.

'Who are you?' you ask, gently.

'Paresh Porob,' he whispers.

You're about to lose all hope, but then you hear a soft chuckle.

'I wanted to be captured. Look at this.' Paresh holds out a tiny silver transmitter. 'Our fellow rangers have tracked me and will soon arrive and catch King Cobra. We'll all be released and can continue our fight for the conservation of the natural environment.'

You smile and grasp his hand.

THE END

You hesitate. Another gunshot forces you to make a decision. You run deep into the forest, as far away as you can get.

You dodge through teak trees that are about forty metres tall. They must be nearly a hundred years old to be that tall. This must be a protected rare old-growth teak forest.

A chainsaw whines in the distance. You don't know whether to run towards it or away. Your legs feel as heavy as teak logs.

If you head towards the chainsaw, turn to page 70
If you keep running, turn to page 71

Chainsaws mean people. You charge towards the sound.

Five men stand around a fallen teak tree. You hear another chainsaw nearby.

'What are you doing?' you shout.

They watch you approach, standing as still as mannequins.

'Don't you know this is illegal?' you scream.

They look down at the ground and shuffle their feet. One whispers something into a two-way radio.

'Answer me!' you say.

One of the men walks towards you and pulls out a piece of cord. 'Sorry, but you must understand. We have families. If we're offered money, sometimes we have no choice but to accept. Even when it is doing something we know is wrong. We are very poor.'

The guy who whispered into the radio yells, 'The boss will pick him up soon.'

'Never!' you scream. You dive back among the teak trees.

A voice yells, 'Stop!'

You ignore it. You feel as if you can run forever.

Somewhere a voice yells *'Timber!'*

A shadow falls across you.

Everything turns black.

THE END

You long to run in the direction of the chainsaw, but you fear whoever is using it might be employed by the fake Paresh.

Soon you start to relax as your body finds its natural running rhythm. You run kilometres. The impostor ranger must be far away by now. You slow down to a jog and observe your surroundings. The trees are thinning out and you spot a trail ahead.

That's funny. You see a rock that looks just like the rock you sat on with the impostor ranger.

You step onto the trail. It is the same rock. You have run kilometres in a huge circle.

'Welcome,' says the supposed Paresh Porob. He holds a large gun.

That's the last thing you ever see.

THE END

You rush towards the sound of the engine. One part of you thinks that you should try to be quiet, but the other part of you thinks you should run for your life.

A bullet slams into a tree just to your right. You veer to the left. The engine sounds loud now. You hope you make it to the track in time. Finally, you break out of the woodland onto the road. You see a jeep.

Hastily, you step back under the cover of the trees. What if the people in this jeep are part of this supposed ranger's gang?

It passes slowly. You see it needs a bit of panel beating, and there's rust on the passenger's door. It's very different from the impostor's jeep. This jeep reminds you of the ranger jeeps back home.

You run out on the road just behind it.

'Help!' you yell.

The jeep stops and a man jumps out. He rushes up to you. 'Can I help?'

Your knees buckle under you and you slump onto the road. All of a sudden your head spins; this is all so confusing.

A strong hand grabs yours and heaves you up. 'Are you okay? I'm Paresh Porob.'

You repeat, 'Paresh Porob.'

'Yes,' he regards you with a puzzled look. 'You've heard of me?'

'I've just escaped a fake you.'

Turn to page 73

Paresh frowns. 'I don't understand. You wear a ranger's uniform.'

'You wrote an email to me,' you say.

'It's you?' He smiles as widely as a dolphin. 'I feared you were yet another missing ranger. I felt so guilty because I invited you here. Oh, it is so good to meet you.'

A gunshot, then another, and yet another rings out.

'Oh dear,' says Paresh. 'If I'm not mistaken, those gunshots come from three different guns. One or even two gunmen we could face, but three? Let's go and regroup. We'll return with reinforcements and sort out my impersonator.'

You both jump into the jeep and Paresh speeds off. 'Come, you must tell me your story,' he says.

Twenty minutes later you arrive at the ranger camp. The gates are wide open.

Paresh frowns. He toots the horn. 'Hello!' he shouts.

Silence. The camp is deserted.

Paresh's eyes are red, as he examines the marks on the dirt driveway.

'Five rangers. All gone. Look, you can see they were dragged to a ...' He squats and peers at the tyre tracks. 'It looks like a large truck; see here,' he points, 'it had six sets of wheels, it drove in and took away the rangers as if they were sheep.'

73

Turn to page 74

The two of you walk through the living quarters. Chairs are overturned. Sausages and eggs congeal half eaten on a plate.

'They've all disappeared,' murmurs Paresh. 'I can't believe this.'

You think hard. 'Someone knew you were picking me up at the hospital today and must have told the fake Paresh. Who knew?'

'No-one except the other rangers and the hospital. They contacted me when they found my email among your papers.'

'So someone, either a person at the hospital or a ranger, knew you wouldn't be here.' You stop; you can hear something, a sort of high-pitched hiss from the door labelled OFFICE.

Paresh opens the door and stops. A king cobra more than six metres long draws itself up until its head is level with the top of the door. Its hood spreads wide.

A small, furry, very fat animal with a long tail and short rounded ears launches itself at the snake. The cobra slides down and slithers past you.

Paresh grabs the mongoose and pats it. 'Well done, George. Cobras fear a mongoose because it's speedy and agile, its thick fur protects it from bites and it attacks cobras. Our enemy left us a warning. It's King Cobra. I've heard rumours of where he's based; let's go there.'

Turn to page 76

74

Driving in the jeep, you smell the beautiful fragrance of the trees before you see them. You look down the mountain side; sandalwood trees spread as far as you can see.

You hear the whine of a chainsaw. Paresh frowns and tilts his head. 'There's no government-approved logging here.'

You know that sandalwood forests are extremely endangered and government-owned in India. 'King Cobra?' you ask.

'I fear so,' answers Paresh. 'How are you at sneaking up on people?'

You and Paresh dodge through the trees until you near three men standing around a fallen tree. You suck in your breath. He's there, the fake Paresh Porob, aka King Cobra.

'Get going, you lazy fools,' yells King Cobra. 'If I were you, I would be more worried about *this* King Cobra than some myth.'

A man puts down his chainsaw. 'It's well known that sandalwood trees attract cobras; they wrap themselves around the trunk to be near the smell.'

The other man hands his chainsaw to King Cobra. 'It's true, and we did find that king cobra this morning.'

'You should be more scared of this King Cobra.' He draws out a gun. 'If you're not going to be helpful you can join those interfering rangers.'

Turn to page 77

Paresh exchanges a glance with you. Together you follow King Cobra as he pushes the two men in front of him and marches them away.

'Get in there,' he orders. He unlocks a barred gate over a pit and shoves the men inside.

'Fools,' he mutters. He marches back to the fallen tree and picks up a chainsaw. His hand is about to flick the 'on' button when there's a huge roar.

Paresh mouths, 'Tiger.'

You glance around, but you know it's unlikely to be nearby, and that a tiger's roar can be heard from three kilometres away.

You're wrong. A Bengal tiger winds its way through the sandalwood trees only metres away. You freeze.

King Cobra starts and picks up his camera. It's dark in the forest and you know what will happen if he takes a photo.

'Stop!' you yell. Tigers are known to attack if frightened by a camera flash.

'*You!*' he roars, almost louder than the tiger. 'I'll deal with you in a moment, but first I want to take a photo of this tiger. People are strangely squeamish, so I think I might advertise the animal for sale with a living photo.'

'Don't do it,' orders Paresh.

Turn to page 78

From page 77

King Cobra looks at him blankly. 'Why ever not? You do know I'm pointing my camera and not my gun. I'll use that once I take an action photo.'

He takes the photo and the whole forest lights up with the flash. The tiger roars and pounces on King Cobra.

You and Paresh manage to frighten the tiger off, but it's too late for King Cobra.

'It is a waste,' says Paresh, as you look at King Cobra's body.

'What about grabbing the keys? That's something we can do,' you say.

You unlock the iron gate over the pit, and you and Paresh help the people out. Most wear tattered ranger uniforms.

'Deepak! All of you,' yells Paresh. 'You're back!'

That night you all party at the ranger camp. Even George the mongoose wears a ranger hat. The next morning you wake up to a surprise.

'Hey Paresh,' you say.

'Hmm.' He's still half asleep.

'Did you notice George was a little chubby? Look.'

Seven baby mongoose squirm inside the ranger hat.

Paresh laughs and strokes the adult mongoose.

'Whoops. Kids, I want to introduce you to your mum, Georgina.'

THE END

From page 6

You could follow Mr Gupta and the young guy, but chances are you'll all meet up outside the toilet at the end of the carriage, so you decide not to.

'Fortescue Station,' booms a voice from the public address system.

You shove the business card into your pocket, grab your hat and backpack, and step carefully over the sleeping bodies to the carriage door. You sidle past the crowd in the corridor. One family sits around a blue-and-white checked tablecloth. The mother, wearing a red sari, holds up a plate of yellow puffs of pastry as you shuffle past.

'Samosas,' she says as she offers it to you.

79

It would be rude not to accept. 'Thank you very much,' you say. Your teeth crunch into crisp pastry, showering the little boy squatted by your feet. He frowns and throws you an evil look, but his mother shakes her head at him so he keeps quiet.

You don't care what he was going to say. Your tastebuds are in heaven. You taste curry, potatoes and spices: it's so yummy you want to grab the entire plate and gobble up the lot. That would give the little boy something to grumble about.

'That was delicious,' you say.

Turn to page 80

From page 79

'Join us,' says the father, pointing to an area on the floor about five centimetres wide. You couldn't even fit your boot there. This corridor is seriously packed.

'Sorry, I'm getting off.' You smile and walk to the exit door. You don't pass either Mr Gupta or the young guy. The toilets near the exit door are both occupied.

You shrug. Looks as if you were right about where Mr Gupta and the young guy would be. The train slows down and you wait for it to stop. You don't need to hold on to the overhanging strap because people are packed so tightly around you that there's no danger of falling.

80

Turn to page 81

You're the only one to get off the train. Outside, the warm air blankets you. You stretch; it's such a relief to be able to walk and lift your arms without knocking anybody.

It's early morning, but already the sun scorches you. Everything appears bleached: the long tan-coloured grass, the pale-pink brick train station and the dusty dirt road.

It's deserted, except for one dilapidated taxi that looks like if you kicked it once, all the wheels would fall off.

You sigh. This must be your lift to the ranger camp. You approach the ancient-looking driver. He spits a purple leaf through the broken window onto the dusty track right near your foot and smiles. His teeth are stained purple.

You hear the sound of a motor somewhere behind you.

'Hey!' a voice yells out. 'Old man, no spitting betel nuts at visitors. That's disgusting.'

Turn to page 82

From page 81

A young guy with gleaming white teeth climbs out of a three-wheeled motorised rickshaw. He strides towards you, and holds out his hand. 'I'm Jai. Sorry I'm late; I'm here to take you to the ranger camp.'

The taxi door creaks open and the driver stumbles out, leaning on a walking stick. 'I sit and wait here every day. I take the rangers to the camp. It's always been so.'

You glance at the taxi's seat and wince. At least two evil-looking springs pierce the cracked red leather. And the taxi driver must be one hundred years old. Is it safe for a centenarian to drive you?

The brand-new motorised rickshaw shines. And, unlike the taxi driver, Jai looks as if he'll stay awake for the trip.

Who should you go with?

*If you choose to go with the ancient taxi driver,
turn to page 84*
*If you choose to go with the young guy in the motorised rickshaw,
turn to page 114*

'Come on, I'll take your bag,' says Jai, grabbing it.

The taxi driver remains silent.

'Hurry up,' shouts Jai as he flings your bag into the motorised rickshaw.

'I wonder why this hurry?' murmurs the taxi driver.

'I wonder, too,' you say. Jai's being a bit too pushy.

You glance at the taxi driver. He may be more wrinkled than your fingers after they've been submerged in water for an entire day, but his brown eyes are sharp.

Jai slams his hand on the horn and starts up the motor.

You rush to the rickshaw and snatch your bag out of it. 'I'll catch the taxi.'

'No, you're not!' shouts Jai. 'I'm meant to pick you up.'

The taxi driver swings open the passenger door. He places a red, yellow and orange embroidered velvet mat carefully over the broken springs and you jump in.

Jai reaches your door as the taxi starts. 'Wait!'

You don't want to offend anyone. 'You can pick me up on my way home.'

Jai says nothing, but grips the doorhandle.

'Let go. You'll get hurt,' you say.

Jai clenches his fist. He's not letting go.

'Don't worry,' says the taxi driver. 'This car was designed for these emergencies.'

Turn to page 85

The taxi eases forward and Jai flops back on the dirt road, still holding the doorhandle in his fist.

You gasp.

'My cousin supplies me with cheap doorhandles,' says the taxi driver. He frowns in the rear-vision mirror. 'Observe our young friend back there.'

Jai stands in the middle of the road. He doesn't seem hurt or angry; he looks scared.

'I've never met Jai,' says the taxi driver. 'He doesn't come from around here. The rangers know I, Noel, always meet the train.'

'So who sent him?' you ask.

'We could always follow him if that's what you wish,' says Noel.

You know you should report to Paresh Porob straightaway, but what if this is your only chance to try and find out who sent Jai to pick you up and why?

If you decide to follow Jai, turn to page 86
If you decide to go straight to the ranger camp,
turn to page 145

'I want to follow him,' you say, 'but he'll know the taxi.'

'A mere minor detour and we'll fix that.' Noel cranks up the car. Smoke billows out from under the bonnet as the taxi veers off the dirt track onto an even smaller, dirtier track, and pulls up outside a bright blue house.

Squawking geese fly into the sky and a cow ambles over to your open window. Its brown eyes gaze at you, before its big yellow teeth snap at your shoulder.

'*Ouch*,' you say, but you push the cow's head away gently so you can climb out. The cow is honoured in India as being a sacred beast.

Noel limps with his walking stick across to an old shed made of corrugated iron, and tugs at the wooden door. You join him and yank the door open. It trembles then crashes down on the ground. Whoops. 'I'm sorry,' you mutter.

'Happens every time,' says Noel. He pulls off a tarpaulin to reveal a motorised rickshaw. 'Adapted to my own design. Look.'

The three wheels are thick and wide; they're all-terrain tyres.

'Let's go!' Noel shouts. You jump in and the rickshaw putters across the fields. You stare at a cloud of dust far away on the main road – Jai.

Turn to page 88

Going cross-country is a bumpy ride. Your teeth feel chipped, and as for your brains, they slosh around like a milkshake in your skull as you jerk up and down. Obviously, Noel didn't think fixing the springs was as important as the tyres and a revved-up engine.

Finally, the motorised rickshaw reaches the outskirts of a village. It's market day. People are everywhere, and it's so noisy your ears hurt. You glimpse Jai jumping out of his motorised rickshaw, then he disappears into the crowd.

'He's over there,' you say, pointing.

Noel slows the motorised rickshaw and reaches under his seat. 'There,' he says, thrusting a bundle of orange cloth at you.

'What?' It's a turban, the head covering some Indians wear. 'Is it even right for me to wear this?'

'Of course,' says Noel. 'Men and women, all religions. And certainly not as obvious as your ranger hat.'

You've just fitted the turban when you spy a ranger hat across the other side of the square. 'Hey!' you shout.

Turn to page 89

From page 88

Noel glares at you. 'Shh. You're supposed to be inconspicuous.'

You nearly say that it is highly unlikely anyone would hear you screaming your head off over the loud noise, but you keep quiet as right now Noel looks like a cranky old man, and you have to admit that he does have a point. Basic ranger training: when conducting surveillance, keep a low profile.

You pop on your sunglasses and slump down in the motorised rickshaw, following the ranger hat bobbing through the crowd with your eyes. He or she is tall and moves fast through the swirl of red, aqua, pink and yellow saris. Eventually, you see the ranger hat emerge at the other side of the square. He stands in front of a stall piled high with bananas. Two seconds later Jai slinks up to him.

'A rendezvous,' murmurs Noel.

'Not necessarily,' you say. 'Jai might be hungry. I'm going to creep over and see if I can hear anything.'

'They could be dangerous,' says Noel.

'But it's a ranger,' you say. 'Jai might be threatening him. He could need help.'

If you decide to observe from a distance, turn to page 90
If you decide to try and listen in, turn to page 96

Noel has a point. Better to be cautious for now.

Jai holds out his hand and the ranger bats it away and strides off. Jai follows him for a few steps, then stops. He looks directly across the square in your direction, but his eyes slide past you. The turban disguise is working.

'We may as well go back to the ranger station and get you reported in,' says Noel.

'Hold on,' you say as you spy the ranger hat bobbing through the crowd towards Jai. 'The ranger is back.'

'I wish he would look this way so I could identify him.' Noel screws up his eyes in concentration.

The ranger hands a hessian sack to Jai, who peeks inside and jumps backwards. You're too far away to hear, but his mouth is a perfect ○, as if he's screaming.

90

Turn to page 91

'I wonder what's in that sack,' mutters Noel.

'No idea.' You search the crowd, but you can't find the ranger hat.

'Let's talk to Jai,' you suggest. 'I'll go by myself if you can't manage the crowd.'

Noel gives you a pitying look and stumbles out of the motorised rickshaw. He waves his walking stick. Like magic, a path appears in the crowd and you scuttle behind him, towards Jai.

Jai's at his motorised rickshaw. It's all crushed and dinted, like someone took an axe to it.

'I am so sorry,' says Noel quickly. 'You must let me help.'

Jai shakes his head, tears running down his cheeks. 'They promised me this so I could make a living for my family.'

'We can come to an arrangement. I'll loan you a motorised rickshaw and when you can pay me back, I know you will.'

'Are you sure?' you whisper to Noel.

'We're countrymen, aren't we, Jai? You will not disappoint me,' Noel says loudly.

'What was in the bag? We had you under observation,' you say.

Jai claps his hand over his mouth and shakes his head. His dark eyes are huge with fear.

Turn to page 92

Jai's not going to talk. Maybe if you explain to him that you know something's going on and you won't leave until he tells you what it is ...

Noel slightly shakes his head as if he can read your mind. He's right. Jai slumps to the ground and puts his arms around his legs until he's a ball. Huge sobs shake his body. Noel kneels beside him and pats his back while talking softly.

You poke your head under the crushed roof. A ranger hat lies on the seat. It moves a centimetre. You blink and rub your eyes. You obviously need more sleep. You stare at the hat again.

The hat rises slightly off the seat. This is great. You're here in India to help and you're having hallucinations. You fight the urge to slump on the ground next to Jai. You must be going crazy.

92

Turn to page 93

From page 92

You lean into the wreckage until your head hovers over the ranger's hat. *Ouch*. The hat rises and bops you on the nose. You jump away, rubbing your nose.

You watch the hat rise higher and higher. A graceful creamy-brown snake appears. It tips forward and the hat slides off to reveal the distinctive hood of the Indian cobra, also known as the spectacled cobra. On the rear of the hood you see the two circular ocelli patterns connected by a curved line, resembling spectacles. It is the average length for Indian cobras, 1.9 metres.

You shudder when you think how you nearly kissed a cobra. The Indian cobra is extremely venomous and if bitten, you can die within an hour.

'Noel,' you say, 'we've got a bit of a problem.'

Noel and Jai join you. Jai gasps and points at the cobra. 'He left his calling card. The cobra.'

'King Cobra?' whispers Noel.

Jai nods.

'He is the worst poacher our country has ever seen,' says Noel. 'No-one knows his real identity. He is ruthless and will sell anything and everything, no matter what.'

Jai whispers, 'He even sold his own grandmother.'

Noel smiles a little. 'I too have heard that rumour, but I don't believe it. But if he thought there was a profit to be made, who knows?'

You examine the cobra intently. 'Do you mind?' You point to Noel's stick.

Turn to page 94

Noel nods, and you use the stick to gently prod the cobra. It is as you expected: the cobra's fangs have been ripped out, so it can't bite anyone.

You sense movement in the lane opposite. You race down the lane and skid to a halt when you come face to face with the supposed ranger, who you suspect is King Cobra in disguise. He holds a revolver with a huge silencer attached.

'Welcome, welcome. I'm King Cobra. Why didn't you just come with Jai?'

You don't say a word.

'Not talking?' he asks. 'That's fine. I just want a certain business card. My spy heard my company mentioned, but the fool failed to see who handed the card to you.'

You shake your head and jam your hands in your pockets.

'You're very young. I'm not totally without conscience. Give it to me and I'll let you go.'

Turn to page 95

You stare at the revolver.

'If you don't hand it over, I'll just shoot you and take it,' he says calmly.

What choice do you have? You pull out Mr Gupta's card and memorise the telephone number. As soon as you get away, you can warn him about what you've done.

King Cobra grabs you by the neck and squeezes tightly.

'What are you doing?' You can barely talk.

'How much will you pay me to let you go?' he asks.

'I haven't got any money now ...' you whisper. 'When I go to the ranger camp ...'

'Too late. You're worth more to me dead. Profit is the main thing. Goodbye.'

THE END

You don't trust Jai; he was definitely up to something. The ranger, whoever he is, could be in danger, and you're the ranger to help.

'You stay here, I'll find out what's happening.' You jump out of the motorised rickshaw and dive into the crowd, with Noel's shouts of 'Wait!' ringing in your ears.

Everyone in the world seems to be here. Old, dignified men with long beards wearing white tunics and loose trousers. Old ladies with huge baskets talking and shrieking to each other. Whole families, the women dressed in gaudy gold-embroidered saris, and the children darting in and out of the crowd.

One boy carries a lion-tailed macaque monkey on his back. Its silver-white mane stands out against its black, hairless face. They're an endangered species; only around 2500 still live in tropical dry forests and rainforests.

'Do you realise that your monkey is a member of an endangered species?'

The little boy stares at you and giggles. 'I like your hat.'

You wish you had your ranger's hat, and quickly remove your turban. 'It is illegal to buy a member of an endangered species.'

'We found him. Look, he's injured.' The monkey has a mangled paw, probably from a trap. The boy pokes out his tongue and disappears into the crowd.

Ahead, you spy the ranger hat. Hopefully this is one thing you'll be able to fix.

Turn to page 98

From page 96

Suddenly a loud wail fills the air. You can't see the ranger hat anymore.

'He's down!' a voice shouts.

You push past people, desperate to help the ranger; rangers are all part of one big family. 'Sorry,' you mutter as you stand on someone's foot; 'Whoops,' you say as you accidentally elbow someone in the ribs. Finally you join the semicircle of hushed people staring down at the cobblestones.

A body sprawls on the ground. His ranger hat is squashed under his head.

A hissing two-metre cobra is coiled on the ground and slowly crawls along an outstretched arm onto his chest.

'Keep calm,' you say. 'You'll be safe now I'm here.'

The ranger rolls his eyes towards you.

'Sshhh,' you whisper. 'Remember, you must keep still and quiet so you do not appear to be a threat. Soon the cobra will slither off and leave you.'

The cobra raises the front third of its body and elongates its neck until its hood forms. It's in classic attack pose. The cobra has relatively small fangs and isn't muscular, so instead it tries to bluff and intimidate any predators.

Turn to page 100

'Keep still,' you murmur. 'Once it knows you're not a threat, it will calm down.'

The ranger flickers one eye slightly.

The cobra stays poised in attack mode with its hood outstretched.

'I can't keep still any longer,' whispers the ranger through the corner of his mouth. He keeps his lips motionless so there is no movement to startle the snake.

'Yes, you can,' you say.

'Come a little closer so I can see you properly. I won't feel as alone,' he mumbles. 'You'll be safe. I'm the one in the strike zone.'

You leave the shelter of the crowd and slide your feet closer, being sure not to make any jerky moves. You gaze down into the ranger's eyes. He's a brave man. If it was you, you would be sweating or shivering.

He winces slightly. 'Take your sunglasses off, the sun's reflection hurts my eyes.'

It's not that sunny, and you purchased a special pair of sunglasses that are meant to be non-reflective, for when you observe animals and don't want them to be aware of your presence. Still, the poor guy must be terrified, even if he doesn't look it.

If you remove your sunglasses, turn to page 101
If you decide to leave your sunglasses on, turn to page 105

If it makes him happy ... You raise your hand and slowly push your sunglasses onto the top of your head. The crowd murmurs its approval.

In one fluid movement the ranger yanks your ankle. You catch a glimpse of a huge king cobra tattoo on each hand, before you stumble to your knees and land just behind his head on the cobblestones.

Ouch! Your eyes, your eyes! The cobra squirts two jets of venom directly at you. Typical defensive behaviour. You roll on the ground in agony. The ranger sprints off.

'Help me!' you cry. You force yourself to peer through one eye, despite the stinging pain. Fuzzy images waver in front of you, but at least you're not blind.

101

You hear a hubbub of voices, 'The cobra spat right in the eyes', 'the venom jets were about two metres, it was incredible'. It doesn't feel incredible. The pain is almost unbearable. The cobra venom feels like acid. White pain drills into your eyes.

Turn to page 102

At last, the sound of running feet and a cool hand on your forehead. You feel a prick in your arm. Someone squirts something in your eyes and a voice says, 'The fluid will soothe your eyes and stop more damage to the corneas until we reach the hospital.'

Soft cotton pads and a loose bandage are placed over your eyes. It's a relief, as it cuts out the light, which is murder. In moments you're in the back of an ambulance.

'You're lucky, you know,' says a voice. 'My partner and I were attending a corpse nearby in the market square. He was killed by a knife in the heart.'

Your heart pounds. 'What did he look like? Was he a ranger too?'

'No. Don't freak out, but he's actually lying beside you. If only you could open your eyes, you might be able to help us identify him.'

'No need for that,' says a voice you haven't heard before. 'I checked his ID. He's Jai Fernandez.'

Dread fills your stomach. 'You didn't see a ranger?'

'No rangers except for you. I'm guessing by the uniform that you're a ranger despite the orange turban?'

You nod. He continues talking but you don't hear him. The fake ranger wanted Jai dead and you blinded. Why?

Turn to page 103

From page 102

You wake up and stare at the ceiling. Phew, you're not blind. You were stupid to remove the sunglasses. You feel stupid to have been fooled by that supposed ranger.

'It's hard for an honourable ranger such as you to recognise that another ranger may be a fake.' You know the voice. It's Noel. How could he tell what you're thinking?

'You talk a great deal in your sleep,' he says, once again demonstrating his uncanny ability to mind-read. 'The ranger's been caught. Paresh Porob suspects he's King Cobra, the master criminal all of you rangers have chased for ages, but we have no proof of his identity.'

You smile. 'I should have guessed. On the train a man drew a king cobra on the back of his business card. I'm to contact him if I need help. I think he'll help us identify this King Cobra. But what about Jai? I feel terrible about him.'

'I've visited his family, and his younger brother will drive one of my motorised rickshaws with an agreed splitting of the profits. We'll both do well out of the deal.'

Turn to page 104

From page 103

'Wait until I identify this King Cobra in court,' you declare. 'He wanted the cobra to spit in my eyes so there was no risk of my being able to identify him.'

'He might claim you can't identify him because of possible eye damage.'

'Well, hopefully we'll have Mr Gupta from the train, and what if I identify a certain tattoo of a king cobra on his hands? I'll remember his face forever. I stared into it and thought what a brave ranger he was,' you say.

'You'll prove yourself the bravest ranger of all if you testify against him.'

'I thrive on danger.' A part of you shivers at the thought of what he might do to try to stop you. But it will all be worth it when you have your day in court and justice is done.

THE END

From page 100

You start to push your sunglasses up onto your head, but decide against it. There's one very frightened cobra here, and you need every bit of protection you can use.

Suddenly, something yanks your ankle. You look down and see the ranger's hand while at the same time you stumble forward. Cobra venom squirts your eyes.

The crowd murmurs '*Ooohhhh*' as you collapse back on your bottom. The venom drips harmlessly off your sunglasses. You shake uncontrollably, thinking about what would have happened if you hadn't been wearing your sunglasses.

The ranger jumps up, grabs the cobra, then runs off through the crowd.

'Stop him!' you yell, but it's useless. Who would approach him with his snake?

105

Turn to page 106

You hear a *put-put* sound. Noel's motorised rickshaw parks beside you. 'Are you ready to go to the ranger's camp now?'

You nod wordlessly and allow him to help you climb onto the seat. 'Thanks.'

He smiles. 'I like to help.'

'Why?'

'Many years ago, when I was even younger than you, I accompanied the hunters on their trips. I was proud to be a gun bearer. Every morning I used my knowledge of the land to find leopards, tigers, lions, rhinoceros, everything. The hunters rewarded me. Now I see no tigers; lions are rare. Every time a tiger dies, a part of India is killed.' His old eyes look sad and he sighs. 'But now I make amends. Paresh Porob understands.'

106

Turn to page 107

From page 106

The motorised rickshaw putters into the ranger camp and a tall man runs out.

'I feared you weren't coming. I'm Paresh Porob.'

A huge hand squeezes yours. You wiggle your fingers to check nothing is broken.

'I really was starting to fear another missing ranger,' says Paresh.

'You nearly had one,' you say. You and Noel tell him about Jai and how the fake ranger tried to get the cobra to spit in your eyes.

'I fear it was King Cobra,' says Noel. 'You know the rumour that he controls cobras. This impostor ranger knew well the habits of cobras. He kept still, and it was only when he pulled down our friend here that the cobra attacked.'

'Would you know him if you saw him again?' Paresh asks you.

'Yes.' You'll never forget that face. You stared into his eyes and thought how brave he was, when all the time he planned to harm you.

Turn to page 108

'The problem is, where do we find him?' says Noel.

That man on the train, Mr Gupta. 'I think I know who we can ask.'

You explain your meeting with Mr Gupta, and how he squiggled the picture of the king cobra on the back of his card. 'He wore a green string on his wrist.'

Paresh and Noel both hold out their wrists. 'Like this,' they say together.

You nod.

'This may be the stroke of luck we've long hoped for. This string is worn by those who support the aims of rangers throughout the world. I'll ring this Mr Gupta now,' says Paresh.

108

Turn to page 109

From page 108

Your collar scratches your neck, and the smart shoes pinch your toes. 'Is this really necessary?' you ask.

Paresh and Noel, who both wear suits, nod. Paresh explains, 'Mr Gupta has arranged for us to attend the general meeting of the Axco Trading Company, one of the richest companies in the world, where we can confront King Cobra. If we can convince the shareholders of his company that King Cobra is a poacher, half our battle will be won. They won't let us in unless we look like shareholders. You can pretend that Noel is your grandfather.'

Noel parks the taxi outside a huge building made of white marble. Your shoes squeak as you walk across the entrance. Paresh looks about twice his size with a sack hidden under his tightly buttoned suit coat, and Noel squeezes his walking stick.

109

The three of you pause at the door of the conference room. 'Ready?' asks Paresh.

Turn to page 110

You nod and slide into one of the seats at the back of the room. You gasp when you look down to the front. 'I'm happy to announce yet more record profits,' announces King Cobra. He wears a suit and thin white cotton gloves, but you would know him anywhere.

'Stop!' shouts Paresh.

The audience gasps.

'If you've got something to say, spit it out,' says King Cobra.

'This man here, he is a disgrace to all India,' says Paresh.

A voice shouts out, 'If he makes a profit, I for one can live with the disgrace.'

King Cobra bows slightly, and the audience titters.

Turn to page 111

'Well, what about this?' shouts Paresh. He unbuttons his coat and a sack falls to the ground. You pick it up and the three of you stride to the front of the room.

'*Ooohh*. I'm so scared,' says King Cobra. 'I hope this is going to make money. We all want to make a profit.'

'Even from this?' you say, holding up a tiger skin. Its orange skin with black stripes glows under the fluorescent lights.

'*Agghhh*,' groans the audience.

King Cobra pretends to examine the skin. 'A very old tiger. Probably died from old age.'

'Not only is the skin sold, but even the teeth and the bones. Some people believe that if you have these you'll gain the strength of the tiger,' says Paresh.

A woman stands up. 'I didn't know we made money from things like this.'

'By supporting your owner here,' Paresh points to King Cobra, 'you condone the killing of tigers, leopards, and not only animals; our sandalwood forests are being destroyed. You need to decide: is it worth it? Is the money or the tiger worth more to you?'

Someone starts to clap. 'Well done,' says King Cobra. 'I planned to bring this to everyone's attention today, but you've saved me with your somewhat theatrical performance.'

You can't believe he said that!

Turn to page 112

'But, it's all your fault,' you say. 'It's people like you who encourage tiger poaching. You only care about profit. And you tried to blind me. I can swear it in a court.'

'Calm yourself, young person,' says King Cobra. 'Now ...'

'You've all heard of King Cobra,' says Paresh. 'This is he.'

'I've never heard of that chap.' King Cobra steps backwards, near a large chest.

'What about the gloves?' Noel thunders.

'I explained before you made your late entrance. A bad case of eczema.'

You pluck off a glove. A tattoo of a king cobra decorates his hand.

'King Cobra!' yells a man in the audience. 'Stop him! He has killed many.'

King Cobra opens the chest and two king cobras glide out, their hoods flaring.

The audience screams and stampedes towards the door.

'Wait!' you yell. You grab Noel's walking stick and pretend to play it like a flute. The snakes writhe and twist in the air as they follow the movement of your fingers.

Soon they slink back down into two loosely coiled balls.

Turn to page 113

From page 112

King Cobra freezes as three policemen march into the room.

'Goodbye, King Cobra,' you say. 'I can't say it's been a pleasure knowing you.'

'Ditto,' he hisses.

Paresh and Noel pat your back. 'What was his real name?' you ask.

They look at you blankly.

A small, smartly dressed man strides up to you. It's Mr Gupta! 'It's on the company prospectus. Apu Bahm.'

You, Paresh and Noel laugh until your sides ache.

THE END

Given the choice of an ancient man driving a car way past its use-by date and a young, alert guy in a brand-new motorised rickshaw, it's the new motorised rickshaw every time. You want to reach the ranger camp this century.

'Sorry,' you tell the taxi driver as you climb into the motorised rickshaw. 'But if the ranger camp sent Jai for me, I'd better go with him.'

The taxi driver frowns and leans against the side of the motorised rickshaw. 'But ...'

Jai thumps down on the accelerator and the motorised rickshaw putters off. The old taxi driver staggers backwards, but manages to keep his balance.

'Hey, maybe ...' you start, then you shrug. No use feeling bad about the old taxi driver, it's done now.

You sit back and gaze at the green countryside. A lone Sarus crane with long spindly crimson legs pecks among the reeds of a muddy stream. It lifts its red head, stares straight at you and makes a trumpeting noise that sounds like a warning. You shiver. It's an old tradition that seeing a crane is an omen; you hope it's not a bad omen.

You give yourself a shake. It's just a bird, even if it is the tallest flying bird in the world. Jai pumps up the radio hanging from the handlebars, and it's all good.

114

Turn to page 116

It gets hotter as the sun climbs higher. You can't wait to have a cool drink at the ranger camp. 'How much further?' you ask. 'I thought the camp wasn't far from the station.'

Jai jumps. 'Um … we'll be there soon.'

He cuts the motor and offers you a sip of water from a plastic bottle. You lift it to your lips and read the words *Axco Trading Company*.

'I met someone who works there.' You pull out the card that the guy in the train gave you. 'A Mr Gupta.'

'I don't know him,' says Jai. 'I've never heard of this Axco Trading Company. I've got to adjust the motorised rickshaw and we'll get going.'

There's no way he hasn't heard of the Axco Trading Company if it's India's biggest company; he even drinks that brand of water. You look at his surly face and decide to keep quiet as he unrolls canvas blinds from the roof. He attaches them to hooks on the outside of the motorised rickshaw. Suddenly, you're closed in on three sides and can only see out the front.

Turn to page 117

From page 116

The rickshaw's motor sputters as the track climbs upwards. Tall mountains lie ahead.

'Do you think we'll make it?' you ask, to start a conversation.

Jai ignores you, but his hands squeeze the handlebars.

With the blinds down, the motorised rickshaw is stifling. Sweat drips down your face and if you're honest, you know it's not only because of the heat: something feels wrong.

'What about letting the blinds open for a bit of air,' you gasp.

'I can't do that. You'll be eaten alive by mosquitoes.'

'But ...' You stop. Jai must know mosquitoes are most active late in the day, and not in the middle of a sunny morning.

'If you're so hot, I'll let down the front blind. That will stop the sun shining in on you. I'm the only one who needs to see where we're going.' He reaches back and yanks at the blind. All you see now is Jai's back through a small plastic window behind him.

You feel as if you're in a canvas coffin.

Turn to page 118

From page 117

'You need to relax. Chill and listen to the music, we'll be there soon.' Jai turns up the radio so loudly he wouldn't hear you even if you screamed. You shut your eyes and swallow to stop your ears from popping with the increased altitude.

It hits you. No-one could hear you scream over the roar of music and the engine. No-one would even know you were inside the motorised rickshaw with the blinds down.

Your ears feel like they've exploded as they pop. You must be high up the mountain now. You nudge your elbow against the canvas blind. It stays taut. It's impossible to unhook it from inside.

118

You stare at Jai's back through the small plastic window. You have no definite proof against him, just your instinct.

Turn to page 119

You don't want to stay in the motorised rickshaw any longer. You're not sure what Jai's plan is, but you're sure you won't like it from the way he keeps glancing back at you through the small plastic window.

Carefully, you slide your hand into the pocket of your shorts, touching your pocketknife. You keep your hand inside your pocket and flick your thumbnail against the tip of the blade to try and pull it out.

Suddenly, the music's turned down. You see Jai's frowning face. He's spotted your arm moving.

'Got an itch,' you explain and scratch your arms and legs. 'A flea bit me on the train. I'm so itchy it must be an entire family of fleas, or maybe even lice.'

Jai shrinks away and turns the music up again.

At last you pull out the blade. You poke the pointed end through the material of your pocket and poke it into the canvas. Nothing. You push harder until finally the tip of the blade breaks through.

Gradually, you pull the blade upwards until you make a slit. Your hope is that when you fling yourself against the canvas, it will split.

Turn to page 120

From page 119

The good thing about a motorised rickshaw is that it doesn't go very fast, especially when climbing up a mountain side. Hopefully, when you jump out you won't injure yourself.

You pull your legs up onto the seat so you can catapult out of the side.

You take a deep breath and brace yourself. On the count of five, you'll jump out of the motorised rickshaw. You stare at the slit in the canvas blind.

One ... two ... three ... You stick your arm through the slit.

The motorised rickshaw swerves as Jai slams on the brakes. You're both flung forward. The front blind twirls upwards.

120

Turn to page 121

'Are you mad?' Jai yells over the music. He grips your wrist and pulls a black gun out of his jacket. 'What are you doing?'

You shake his hand off and point at the gun. 'I would be madder if I stayed here with you.'

'But there's a sheer drop here.' Jai looks terrified.

'You would say that, wouldn't you!' you shout.

You shrug on your backpack and crouch on the seat, ready to spring out.

121

If you jump out of the motorised rickshaw, turn to page 122
If you listen to Jai and stay in the motorised rickshaw,
turn to page 142

The canvas rips as you dive through the slit.

Desperately, you search for something to hold onto as you fall off the side of the mountain, but there's nothing. Your legs scrabble for a foothold, but they cycle uselessly in midair. In seconds you'll hit the ground.

Your heart pounds as you frantically search for something to grab.

Slightly to the right of your downward trajectory is a ficus tree growing out of the side of the mountain. And slightly to your left there's a spindly bush.

This is your only chance. Which one should you try to grab?

122

If you grab the tree, turn to page 124
If you grab the bush, turn to page 133

123

You need to be sure whatever you grab will hold your weight. Your choice is easy; you'll grab the ficus tree. They have long and extensive roots.

You stretch out your arms and swing your body to the right.

You just manage to cling on to a branch. You dangle over ... well, you're not sure what's below because it's covered by clouds, but at least you've stopped falling.

It's quiet up here, but you're not alone. You flip a tiny beetle off the branch and plan your next move. No way can you hang here indefinitely.

You hear a flapping noise and watch two Sarus cranes emerge through the clouds. They ride upwards on a thermal, an updraft of warm air, then they glide forward and disappear back into the clouds. It seems so long ago that you spied the single Sarus crane when you set out in Jai's motorised rickshaw. You wondered back then if it was an omen.

Turn to page 125

From page 124

A crack tears through the air. You examine the tree.
A jagged split creeps along your branch. You notice
tiny metallic beetles, about the size of a grain of rice,
clustered everywhere. They're identical to the beetle you
brushed off before. You should have realised.

The tree is riddled with wood-eating borer beetles.
The core of the tree must be rotten.

The branch creaks and snaps off with a sound like a
gunshot.

125

Turn to page 126

You plummet down through the clouds ... and splash into a pool of freezing water. You've fallen about ten metres onto a sort of plateau.

Four men stare at you in amazement. A tall man strolls towards you with a huge, wolfish grin on his face. 'Jai dropped you off, I presume. Rather unorthodox, but at least you're here.'

'Who are you?' you ask.

His dark eyes burn into you. 'I am King Cobra.'

The picture of the king cobra that Mr Gupta scribbled on the back of his business card flashes into your mind. Somehow you're sure he did it as a warning.

'Welcome to the land of the missing rangers,' says King Cobra. 'Unfortunately, you won't be meeting the esteemed ranger, Paresh Porob. Your visit to India will be somewhat curtailed.'

Every instinct tells you to flee.

'Any chance of dry clothes?' you ask, pretending to shiver.

King Cobra shrugs. 'Soon you won't care what condition your clothes are in, but no-one can accuse me of not being kind.'

King Cobra turns to his men. 'You all find me very kind and pleasant, don't you?'

They all nod and smile. 'Yes, boss,' says a slim young guy with a wispy beard.

He's the young guy from the train!

Turn to page 127

From page 126

'Ah, you recognise Raj,' says King Cobra. 'Apparently someone who works for my company is telling tales. This fool can't remember the traitor's name, and he couldn't find him on the train. Can you help?'

You close your lips firmly and scowl at King Cobra.

He laughs. 'Yet another noble ranger refuses to give me a simple answer! Raj, give our friend dry clothes and then we'll loosen a few tongues.'

Raj shows you silently to a cave. A minute later a bundle of clothes hits you on the head. Quickly you put on the two jumpers and everything else you can find because if you escape, you know you'll die if you spend a night on the mountain without warm, dry clothing.

Raj returns. 'Boss sent this to babysit you.'

He empties a sack and a king cobra tumbles out. It's olive green with faint yellow bands along its six-metre body. King cobras are shy and prefer to flee than attack, but this is one angry snake. Its hood flares as one-third of its body lifts up and it glides forward. You look up at its head, which nearly brushes the roof of the two-metre-high cave.

You step backwards until you're pressed against the rocks and bushes at the rear of the cave. The cobra's hood flares again and the cave echoes with a continuous hiss that sounds like a growling dog. There's a small gap between it and the wall of the cave.

If you choose to make a break for it, turn to page 128
If you stand still, turn to page 129

From page 127

You know that the venom of the king cobra is not the most deadly of all snakes, but you also know that the seven millilitres of venom that the king cobra injects is enough to kill twenty people.

You're a fantastic sprinter. You always have been. If anyone can get past the snake, you can.

Slowly, you take a deep breath and tense your muscles. In a second the king cobra will be too close for you to be able to make it past.

Now! You charge.

Ouch. Something pricks the back of your leg. Your vision blurs and pain radiates through your body. You try to stagger out of the cave, but you slump to the ground, your limbs paralysed.

You shout and wait. You know in two minutes you'll be in a coma. That villain King Cobra could save you, but will he?

THE END

It's unusual for a king cobra to be so aggressive, despite its threatening appearance. Why is this one so aggressive?

It flashes through your mind that the king cobra is the only snake that builds a nest for its eggs, and it guards the eggs ferociously.

You look behind you and among the bushes and rocks you spot a huge nest formed out of leaf litter. About thirty eggs lie in it.

Oh boy.

You squish yourself against the cave wall as far away as you can from the eggs, and freeze.

Moments tick past and the king cobra slowly wraps itself around its nest.

Quietly you pad away from it and head to the cave entrance.

King Cobra sits on a gold-painted deckchair that resembles a throne. His men squat at his feet.

The plateau is bare of any vegetation except grass, but forest surrounds it.

You dash towards the trees.

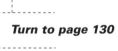

Turn to page 130

From page 129

You made it! You hear shouting but you don't stop. You slide down the mountain, dodging the evergreen trees as you go.

A stitch burns in your side. You crawl into a thicket of bushes and lie panting while you wait for it to disappear.

Suddenly, you're aware that you're not the only one panting. You hold your breath and listen.

Pant, pant, pant.

You examine the bushes and gasp. You see a set of paws.

A voice rings out. 'Found you!'

King Cobra blunders into the bushes. You point at the paws and together you and King Cobra back out of the bushes into the open woodland.

Three tawny-coloured wolves follow you. They're just under a metre in height and all their ribs stick out as if they haven't eaten for a year.

Oh boy. Indian wolves are usually timid, but if they're starving and see fresh meat, aka you and King Cobra, things could get ugly.

Turn to page 132

130

From page 130

You show your teeth and holler. You snatch up a big rock and fling it at them.

'Are you mad?' hisses King Cobra. 'This is how you should act when confronted by wild animals.' He curls into a small ball and lies passively on the grass.

The growling wolves leap on him. King Cobra was wrong. The wolf is one animal that is frightened by aggression.

You shout and whack the animals with a stick and the wolves slink back into the bushes.

It's too late for King Cobra. You mark where he lies dead with twigs so he can be found easily. Then you trudge off to find help and to meet Paresh Porob.

Somehow you know no more rangers will disappear.

THE END

Although the bush appears spindly, it looks tough. It must be tough to grow in this situation. You stretch out your hand.

Contact. The twigs poke into you, but you couldn't care less. Your arms feel as if they're being pulled out of their sockets, but you breathe deeply and try to ignore the pain.

The problem is, what should you do now?

You scan the face of the mountain. About two metres below you spy a narrow ledge and some sort of fissure in the wall. It's too hard to see if it's a cave looking down from above, but at least you would feel safer, rather than dangling from a spindly bush.

You swing your legs a little. If you're lucky you'll be able to swing your legs enough for your body weight to take you towards the ledge, and hope that when you land on the ledge you can balance and not fall off.

But you're okay at the moment hanging from the bush. What happens if you miss the ledge? Maybe you should stay where you are.

If you decide to keep hanging from the bush, turn to page 134
If you decide to try to land on the ledge, turn to page 136

133

From page 133

The ledge looks far away. You're relatively safe now. You can always try to reach the ledge later, when you've had a bit of a rest – although it's hard to rest when your arms are above your head and holding your entire weight.

A cramping feeling creeps up your right thumb and into your fingers. Soon your right hand has lost all sensation. You tighten your grip.

Maybe it's time you did try to land on the ledge. Pain radiates down your right side. It hurts so much, it makes you groan.

Eventually, the pain subsides into numbness, which is a relief.

You swing your body a little, but it feels all wrong because you can't feel your right side and it's hard to get a sense of balancing your weight.

The cramping feeling tingles in your left hand. You don't know how much longer you'll be able hang on.

It's now or never.

Turn to page 135

From page 134

You try to swing your body to the side. It moves slightly.

The whole left side of your body cramps.

You swing your legs and let go of the bush.

You observe the smooth rock face of the mountain as you brush against it. You brace your feet to land on the shelf, but you keep falling.

Desperately, you glance up and see a rocky outcrop just to the right of you. You missed the ledge completely.

You plummet downward, then you don't ever feel anything ever again.

THE END

From page 133

Your arms ache so much, you won't be able to hang on to the bush indefinitely. Who knows how long it will take until you're rescued? You survey the mountain. There's no obvious sign of habitation. Who knows if you'll *ever* get rescued?

You slap yourself mentally. There's no point in worrying about that now.

You decide. You don't want to just hang around waiting; you're going to land on the ledge.

You swing back and forth. Soon your body swings in an arc, each time swinging closer and closer to where the ledge juts out.

Now the tricky part. You'll have to let go when you're at the extreme end of the arc. With a bit of luck, momentum will swing you over the ledge and you'll fall down onto it.

Here goes. You kick your legs back and forth and gradually you gain height.

Time to let go of the bush.

Turn to page 137

From page 136

You did it. You crash onto the rock ledge.

   Pain shoots up your left leg. You force yourself to lift your head and check out your surroundings. A kind of fissure in the rock forms a mini cave. It's no posh hotel, but at least you'll get a bit of shelter. You crawl into it and lie down, and everything grows black.

   You wake up freezing and with a raging thirst. It's snowed. You grab a fistful from the ledge and stuff it in your mouth. It stings, but you don't care. You need water to survive.

Turn to page 138

You stare outside. A vulture circles the ledge. You're lucky to even see one, as vultures are nearly extinct in India; they mainly feed on dead cattle and other livestock, many of which used to be treated with a veterinary drug called diclofenac, which causes kidney failure in vultures. India's banned the drug now, but not before the vulture population was virtually wiped out. It's amazing how much one little thing can affect a whole ecosystem.

Another vulture swoops past. Possibly they're waiting for dinner. You know you're safe for the moment; they only feed on dead animals. Still, you try to crawl deeper into the tiny cave.

138

You cry out suddenly; you've definitely done something to your leg. When you move, the pain in your leg is so agonising that everything fades away.

Turn to page 140

Voices wake you. You open your eyes to see a man and a woman standing on the ledge. Each is equipped with mountain gear. A warm, red thermal blanket covers you.

'Awake at last, Sleeping Beauty. I'm Amita and this is Julian,' says the woman with a smile. A huge pair of binoculars is slung around her neck. 'The helicopter's due any moment.'

You hear a *chop-chop-chop* sound.

'Right on schedule,' she says. 'Don't try and move your leg.'

Of course, as soon as she says that you try and move it. '*Ouch!*' It's excruciating.

She shakes her head. 'I told you not to.'

'How did you get here?' you ask. It's unbelievable that they found you.

'We're ornithologists,' says the man, Julian. 'We were so excited to observe the vultures that we abseiled down the mountain. We did wonder what they were circling, then we heard a moan. Your leg's badly smashed up, but apart from that you're okay.'

Turn to page 141

The helicopter hovers overhead and the next few hours pass in a blur of doctors, hospitals and men in suits who question you repeatedly. You ask to speak to Paresh Porob, or even your rescuers Amita and Julian, but you find yourself placed in isolation.

It doesn't make sense. People can't catch a broken leg. You suspect that someone doesn't want you to speak to rangers, or anyone who values the natural environment.

The next day, you're sent home by emergency evacuation. The first thing you do is switch on your laptop and email Paresh Porob. You say, 'I don't know why they want to keep me away, but I'll return, even if I have to walk over Mount Everest to reach you.'

He emails straight back. 'I will meet you there, my friend. We will fight on.'

THE END

Jai leans towards you with the gun. Your breath catches in your throat. Goosebumps carpet your entire body.

'*Aghhh*,' you gurgle. Your brain is telling you to yell but your voice won't work. It's like one of those dreams when the monster chases you and you want to scream, but you can't.

Jai reaches over you, pushes the barrel of the gun into the slit and tears the canvas blind. It flaps open.

142

Turn to page 143

From page 142

You clutch your seat as your head spins. Black spots float in front of your eyes as you stare at the vertical drop just two centimetres away from the edge of the motorised rickshaw. You're up so high that wisps of clouds float in the valley below.

You just escaped certain death.

'Are you crazy?' asks Jai. 'You want to jump down there?'

You gulp. There's not even a tussock of grass you could grasp to try and stop falling. A weird noise buzzes in your brain and suddenly you're conscious of someone breathing heavily. It takes a few seconds for you to realise it's you.

'This was meant to be easy,' mutters Jai. 'Pick you up, drop you off at the caves and I keep the brand-new motorised rickshaw. No-one said you were a lunatic. Look at you, shivering and panting like a mad dog with rabies.'

'Perhaps.' Your voice squeaks but at least you can talk now. 'Maybe if you pulled the rickshaw away from the side of the mountain, and if you stopped waving that gun around ...'

Jai stares at the gun, then he drops it as though it's a lit match. 'They gave it to me, and I didn't tell them I've never used one in my life.'

Turn to page 144

143

From page 143

'Who are "they"?' you ask.

Jai stares down at his huge, brand-new boots.

'They gave you the boots as well ...?' you ask.

He nods. 'Please understand. My family has nothing. We share a mud hut with one other family. I sleep outside with the dogs to escape everyone. This is the first new pair of boots I've had. And the motorised rickshaw would provide a good living. I'm not much older than you. What would you do if someone made you an offer like that?'

'I would say no,' you say quickly, but you wonder if you would. 'I *hope* I would say no.'

Jai watches you pick up the gun. 'You can't touch that!' he yells. 'You just don't get it. King Cobra owns the Axco Trading Company, which owns half of India. You rangers interfere. He wants to stop you. It's simple. I'm meant to take you to his hideaway.'

'You know where it is?' you ask.

'Obviously, if I'm taking you there.'

'Take me back to the ranger camp. Then I can tell Paresh Porob and we can stop King Cobra. Now I know everything I'll be able to solve the mystery of the missing rangers.'

'Give me the gun then,' says Jai. He leaps on you, and the two of you wrestle.

The motorised rickshaw slowly rolls forward and topples over the edge of the mountain.

You join the ranks of the missing rangers.

THE END

'No, I should report to the ranger camp.'

'It was only a suggestion,' murmurs Noel.

You're not sure, but he sounds hurt. As if a hundred-year-old man would be capable of helping you. What would he do, hit the baddies with his walking stick? And he could only do that if they stood still.

You want to laugh, but instead you say, 'I don't think so, better to go to straight to the ranger camp to tell the other rangers. I'm to meet Paresh Porob.'

'Paresh Porob is a man of action,' says Noel. 'He'll do something.'

Suddenly you wish you had followed Jai, but it's too late now. Anyway it's better to wait for proper trained assistance, rather than rely on an old taxi driver.

Noel slows down even more – it's hard to believe that's even possible. You look ahead and gasp.

Turn to page 146

From page 145

Three black buck antelopes leap and bound around the taxi, before they race off at lightning-fast speed. You just have time to note the distinctive white rings around their eyes and their snow-white bellies before they disappear. You feel lucky that you saw them as they're an endangered species, even though they once roamed the plains of India in huge herds. You'll never understand how people can illegally poach and kill animals.

Three elephants march majestically alongside the road. They keep perfect time with the taxi, so even though the speedo is broken, you can estimate your speed. The normal walking pace for Indian elephants is approximately six and a half kilometres per hour; that explains why this trip is taking forever.

Finally, the taxi rumbles over a cattle grid into the ranger station. You hold out a wad of rupees.

'Go.' Noel waves the money away. 'You're a ranger. You help my country. I've enough money for today and if I need more I'll charge you double fare next time.'

He lifts a hand in farewell. He has a green string around his wrist like Mr Gupta's.

'Wait!' you yell, but he doesn't hear you over the engine. He turns the car around and disappears in a cloud of dust.

A ranger of average height rushes out of the building.

Turn to page 148

From page 146

The man smiles and shakes your hand. 'Just in time for the briefing, my friend. I am Paresh Porob.'

You shake his hand and join six other rangers sitting in a large room.

Paresh holds up a large picture of a smiling man in a ranger hat. 'This is Deepak, the fortieth ranger to disappear this year. We have no information. Nothing. Traces of blood were on the front seat of his abandoned jeep.' Paresh stops and clears his throat.

You feel sick. You know what this probably means.

Paresh looks directly at you. 'Your taxi driver found the car. Noel has long been a good friend to us.'

That old man?

'I'm making a secret journey,' says Paresh. He looks at you. 'It could be dangerous; will you accompany me?'

You gulp, but nod. After all, you are the ranger in danger.

Turn to page 149

148

From page 148

The plane circles over the tall, snow-covered mountains – the Himalayas. Paresh Porob clears his throat. 'I have a big request to ask of you. Our enemy is known as King Cobra. He has a king cobra tattoo on each of his hands.'

Your stomach gripes and the image of a cobra swirls in your brain. 'I met this man on the train, Mr Gupta. He gave me his business card with a cobra squiggled on the back. I think it was a clue.'

'Can you remember who he worked for?' asks Paresh.

'The Axco Trading Company.'

Paresh bites his lip. 'It's worse than I feared. It's one of the world's most powerful companies, and is based in India. If King Cobra is involved with it, we're indeed in trouble. It trades everything. If an item can be sold, it will be sold, whether or not it's an endangered species. Profit is all that matters.'

'Let me help,' you say.

'What do you know about working a camera?'

'Nothing fancy,' you say.

'Many snow leopards were poached this season. There's a rumour that a documentary crew filming snow leopards is a fake, and is actually a group of poachers. If you could work for a documentary crew, you could report any rumours directly to me.'

He hands you a small disc. 'It's a transponder. Pop that in your sock and I'll be able to track you anywhere. And take the two-way radio for contact as well.'

Turn to page 150

From page 149

The jeep drops you off at a camp at the base of a tall mountain.

'Did the agency send you to work the camera?' asks a tall man.

'Yes.' You stretch out your gloved hand, but then let it drop awkwardly to your side when the man ignores it. 'Your name?' you ask.

'Call me Hillary,' he says after a few seconds. 'But you look kind of young; can you even use a camera?'

'Of course.' You know how to hold a camera, and it's just pressing a button. Hopefully he won't have to see the results.

He grunts and points to an enormous backpack. 'We'll see how you do. Carry this while we climb the mountain.'

The backpack weighs a tonne. You didn't know a camera could weigh this much, but you keep your mouth shut and struggle up the mountain after the five men who are the crew.

'Stop,' announces the tall man. 'I'm hot; we'll rest a minute and have a drink.'

He peels off his woollen gloves. You blink. You can't believe it.

A tattoo of a king cobra decorates each hand.

If you radio Paresh straightaway, turn to page 151
If you decide to observe further, turn to page 152

From page 150

What a fantastic stroke of luck! You've been dropped with the fake documentary crew! You need to contact Paresh straightaway.

You look around and see a rock a bit further up the mountain. 'I might go and check the view up there,' you announce to the crew.

They all grunt and you climb up to the boulder. You slide behind it and pull out your radio. '... Paresh. Great to talk to you. You sound as if you're just in front of me. You won't believe this. Guess who the leader of the documentary crew is?'

'King Cobra,' a voice answers.

You look up to see him standing on top of the rock.

'For future reference, not that you will have any future, check the direction the wind blows so your voice doesn't carry downwind to the exact person who you don't want to hear you.'

'I was just talking to a friend,' you say.

'I can believe that. But is it the kind of friend that is good for me? I don't think so.'

He slips a small pistol out of his jacket pocket.

THE END

You fight the temptation to contact Paresh, and instead join the crew and drink tea sweetened with condensed milk.

You hike for a couple more hours. Your legs ache and it's just lucky your back is attached to your body, or it would break off. The backpack is so heavy that everything hurts.

Finally, King Cobra halts again and points to a pile of rocks. 'That's where they're meant to be.'

You join him and look down into a crevice.

Four baby snow leopards are curled up in a den. 'Film them,' commands King Cobra.

You point the camera at the cubs.

'You're very fast,' says King Cobra with a frown.

'I'm known as "one shot". I always say time is money.'

King Cobra nods approvingly. 'I need to film them so we can put the vision of them up on the website. We can hold an auction.' He stops. 'Oh dear, here comes trouble.'

A female snow leopard stands on a rock just above you. It moans. You remember snow leopards can't roar, but it still gives you a fright.

Turn to page 153

King Cobra deftly pulls out a rifle from his backpack and fits it together. 'We don't want any trouble from Mummy.'

You jump up and swipe the rifle out of his hands. It clatters onto rocks far below.

'Oh, whoops,' he says. 'Lucky, I've still got this to deal with you.' He aims a small pistol straight at you. 'Who exactly are you?'

'A ranger, here to defend the natural environment from people like you.'

'*Oooohh*. You rangers are so *scary*.' He laughs. 'I'm not a wicked man, merely a businessman. I sell different products. People buy them. It's all the same to me, whatever I sell. Everything has a price. What a shame no-one is prepared to pay anything for you.'

153

You dive to your left and skid down the side of the mountain. Gravel flies everywhere as a bullet buries itself in the mountain side where your hand was a millisecond ago.

Turn to page 154

You don't let yourself think of King Cobra and his gun.
You need to escape.

Finally you stop, stumbling onto a path. Your foot
hurts, but you force yourself to run on, even though you
limp badly.

Ahead you see a cave; a man with white robes, a
white turban and a long white beard sits cross-legged at
the entrance. He beckons to you. What's he doing in the
middle of a mountain by himself? You've heard of gurus
or holy men who become hermits. But can he be trusted?

154

If you keep running, turn to page 156
If you go to the cave, turn to page 157

From page 154

You run on. The sooner you get off this mountain, the better.

Pain shoots up your leg every single time you place your foot on the ground. You grit your teeth and force yourself to keep moving.

A piece of stone shears off the rock face in front of you. A second later you hear the rifle shot. One part of your brain observes that it really is true: light does travel faster than sound. But the rest of your brain wants to burst into tears and lie down and sleep, and feel no pain.

You shuffle on.

A bullet ploughs into the path just near your foot. You're showered in gravel.

You breathe deeply and continue.

Something stings your calf. You glance down. You're surprised to see a patch of blood growing bigger and bigger.

Ahead you see a flattish rock. You just need to rest for a second, then you'll run away twice as fast. You stagger to the rock and lie down.

You'll get up in a minute ...

THE END

You don't have many choices. Your foot throbs and it's only a matter of time until it won't bear your weight at all. You can't picture yourself hopping off the mountain.

The guru beckons to you again. You limp up to him. 'Hello, I'm a ranger ...'

He holds a finger to his lips and shakes his head. He gestures for you to enter the cave and go behind him.

You lie on the floor of the cave and he flings a length of white material over you.

Seconds later you hear voices. 'Have you seen a young person dashing past?' booms King Cobra.

You lift a corner of the material and peep out.

The guru sits in silence.

'Has there been anyone?' asks King Cobra.

The guru says nothing.

'Well, you're a chatterbox of a guru. Come on men,' shouts King Cobra.

Turn to page 158

You hear footsteps tramp off, then a little later you feel a gentle tap on your ankle.

'*Ouch!*' you scream.

The guru motions for you to take off your boot. Your transponder drops out of your sock, but the guru ignores it. With gentle fingers he rubs your foot with herbs and a smelly paste. This must be Ayurvedic medicine, the traditional medicine practised in India.

The next morning your foot's much better. It's amazing.

'*Hellooo*,' shouts a voice.

You flinch and get ready to dive into the back of the cave.

The guru shakes his head and signs for you to wait. 'I had a vision of your arrival.' His voice is gravelly and squeaky, as if he hasn't talked for a long time.

Turn to page 159

From page 158

Paresh Porob hikes into sight.

'Hello!' you shout. 'Hello.'

'The transponder worked,' he says.

'The plan worked,' you say. 'It is King Cobra. He told me at first that his name was Hillary, but it's definitely him. I saw the tattoos and then he admitted it.'

You approach the guru. 'Thank you for all you've done.'

He gazes over the mountains, and you're not even sure he knows you're leaving until he stretches out his hand slightly. His loose sleeve drops back and you see a green knotted string at his wrist, like the one Mr Gupta wore.

'Oh, I see you're one of us,' says Paresh. He holds out his wrist to reveal a green knotted string. 'The mark of those who support rangers and the work we do.'

159

Turn to page 160

From page 159

'Keep up your work,' murmurs the guru. 'All life is special.'

You wish you didn't have to leave; you want to talk with and learn from the guru, but you and Paresh need to find King Cobra. 'One day I'll come and find you,' you tell the guru.

The guru says, 'But you may not find me. That is not the point. We have met now, when it was ordained.'

You climb down from the cave and look back. Fog swirls around your head. You try to see the cave, but it's hidden.

The crack of a rifle shatters the calm.

'Quick,' says Paresh.

The two of you race along the mountain path as fast as you can without falling over the side. The path twists and you nearly cannon into King Cobra, who gazes towards the top of the mountain.

He swings around in a fluid motion and aims the gun at you and Paresh. 'Oh, so we meet again. The wretched snow leopard wants to play peek-a-boo, but not all is lost if I capture you two.'

Turn to page 161

From page 160

You sense movement and glimpse the snow leopard. It sits among a pile of rocks about twenty metres above King Cobra's head. You don't panic as you know snow leopards rarely attack humans.

'Give me one good reason why I shouldn't shoot you both now,' demands King Cobra.

'It's illegal,' says Paresh.

King Cobra roars with laughter. 'Perhaps I should keep you alive as my personal comedian, Paresh.'

He swings the rifle from you to Paresh. 'Eeny meeny miney mo, which of you rangers should be the first to go?'

You watch in amazement as the snow leopard swipes at a rock. It falls over the edge and hits King Cobra's head.

He looks surprised and collapses. Paresh rushes to him.

161

Turn to page 162

From page 161

'He's all right, only unconscious. I'll call for reinforcements, then we'll take him to jail.'

The snow leopard yawns and slinks back up the mountain. You can't believe that just happened.

Paresh holds something out to you. It's a thin green piece of string. 'Tie three knots in it, and when the string breaks off, your wishes will come true.'

You look at the tall mountains with their snowy tops and the deep blue of the sky.

You know what you want, and you're prepared to work to get it. You tie three knots in the string and attach it to your wrist.

162

THE END

GLOSSARY

Amnesia   Partial or total loss of memory

Anaesthetised   When a drug is used to make a person or
                           animal unconscious

Ankus   A long hook used to train elephants

Antivenene   A mixture used to counter the effects of a
                           poisonous snakebite

Ayuverdic medicine   An Indian medical treatment that includes
                           herbs and massage

Betel nuts   The seed of the Areca palm which stains the
                           teeth purple

Borer   A beetle, which feeds on wood

Brandishing   Wave an object about, often as a threat

Chameleon   A lizard that can change its colour. Chameleons
                           have very long tongues, sometimes longer than
                           their own body length. It has a type of suction
                           cup on the tip of its tongue that it uses to
                           capture its prey.

Coma   A deep state of unconsciousness or sleep

Condensed milk   Sweetened evaporated milk

Corpse   A dead body

Guru   A spiritual teacher

ID   A card or badge used to prove identity

Impostor	Someone who pretends to be someone else
Khur	Wild ass, a donkey-like creature with a black stripe along its back
King cobra	The longest venomous snake in the world, growing up to 5.6 metres long. The venom in a single bite could kill up to twelve people. On the outbreak of World War II, the London Zoo killed its huge 5.7 metre long cobra inmate in case the zoo was bombed and the snake escaped. It belongs to the genus Ophiophagus which means snake eater, and its diet is mainly other snakes
Krait	A very venomous, but usually non-aggressive snake
Mahout	Elephant keeper
Nocturnal	Active at night-time
Ornithologist	Someone who studies birds
Peepul tree	A tree with heart-shaped leaves
Renal failure	When kidneys don't work properly
Rosettes	Rose-like markings or blotches on the fur or skin
Sandalwood	A sweet-smelling tree used for many purposes, including carving and medications. It is a protected species
Sarus crane	Bird
Stampede	Sudden flight or movement of people or animals due to panic

Tranquilliser gun	A non-lethal gun that shoots chemical darts making the animal sleep or be very calm so it can be captured without injury
Transponder	An electronic device that receives and transmits electrical signals. The word is a combination of transmitter and responder.
Turban	Traditional headdress made from a long scarf wrapped around the head.
Venom	A poison

The Real
Paresh Porob

Born in Panjim, Goa, India, Paresh Porob has always been fascinated by animals. As a young boy he gained a reputation as a snake catcher in his neighbourhood, and he always longed to be involved with the protection of nature. His dream came true and he is a ranger who fights for the rights of animals and the natural environment. In the last few years he has rescued more than six adult leopards, three leopard cubs, four gaurs (Indian bison), two wild boars, three spotted deers, and a number of monkeys, snakes, civet cats, birds, crocodiles and turtles. He released most of these animals back into the forest as soon as possible.

As shown in the photo above, Paresh Porob's extraordinary efforts as a ranger have been rewarded with the prestigious Sanctuary Asia–RBS Wildlife Service Award 2009.

The Thin Green Line
FOUNDATION

Using profits from his film, *The Thin Green Line*, which has
been shown in more than fifty countries, and from donations
received from people all over the world, Sean Willmore
started The Thin Green Line Foundation.

The Thin Green Line looks after the welfare of rangers'
families where the ranger has been killed in the line of duty,
and supports community conservation projects to prevent
ranger deaths and protect wildlife.

To find out more about The Thin Green Line, or to support
their work on the frontline of conservation, check out
www.thingreenline.org.au

You can join the rangers on The Thin Green Line by
becoming a member, purchasing their Power of One pack
(includes a DVD of the film *The Thin Green Line*, an eco
T-shirt, sticker, calico bag and membership), or simply
donate to support their valuable work.

It's up to you now!

www.thingreenline.org.au

About the Authors

Sean Willmore worked as a ranger on Victoria's Mornington Peninsula, until he found out that rangers around the world were being routinely killed and injured in the course of their duties and felt compelled to do something. He sold his car, remortgaged his house, and took off around the world with his camera. The result was his documentary *The Thin Green Line*, and the foundation of the same name. His efforts to bring attention to, and support, the dangerous work undertaken by these conservation heroes have won him international acclaim.

Alison Reynolds (www.alisonreynolds.com.au) lives in suburban Melbourne, but she often feels she is a ranger in danger. She has a pack of wild dogs, possums tap-dance on the roof all night, and the neighbour's scarily giant rabbits bounce across the front yard. Then there are the cats, bats and marsupial rats. Along with Sean, she loves to choose her own adventures and hopes you do, too!

Book 1

Ranger in Danger
Diablo's Doom

Do you have the courage to be a ranger in danger?
This is the start of your new life.
You have been selected to travel to Africa as a ranger in training.
You can't wait!
Rampaging elephants, charging rhinos, and hungry man-eating
crocodiles …
The adventures start from the moment you get on the plane.
A scarred man with an eye patch sits near you.
Is this the evil poacher, Diablo?
Can you stop this international criminal?
Will you even make it off the plane alive?
You decide your destiny.

Book 2

Ranger in Danger
Hernando's Labyrinth

Do you have the courage to be a ranger in danger?
You decide your destiny.
You're flying into South America as a ranger in training.
You can't wait!
Stinky skunks, gigantic tarantulas, Mayan ruins,
and flesh-eating piranhas …
A mysterious email triggers more adventures.
Someone's threatening the last Pinta tortoise in the world.
Can you save him and stop the evil mastermind, Hernando?
Your fate is in your hands.

www.rangerindanger.com

Book 4

Ranger in Danger
Rapscallion's Revenge

Do you have the courage to be a ranger in danger?
You decide your destiny.
You're off to the top end of Australia in disguise.
Bring on the danger!
Massive crocodiles, hungry sharks, wild pigs …
Can you capture the crocodile hunters,
before they stalk you?
And who is the mysterious Rapscallion?
Your fate is in your hands.

www.rangerindanger.com